# Backfired

Halfway up the hill, Fargo looked back in the direction of the smuggler's wagons and stopped dead. He stood upright, yelling to Goldman at the top of his lungs. The marshal had timed his approach perfectly, coming up behind the outlaws when they least expected it. He had the towering red-haired gunrunner right where they wanted him. But they hadn't counted on Frederickson's clients showing up at that precise moment. An Apache war chief and six braves rode up and saw what was happening, and Goldman didn't have a chance. The chief and his men fired point-blank into the lawman, killing him in a hail of lead.

Fargo then realized his own danger. He had yelled, hoping to save his friend. But Goldman had died, and now the Apaches knew exactly where he was. He lit out, running hard, but Fargo already knew he would lose the race—the race to stay alive.

# THE
# TRAILSMAN
## #234

# APACHE DUEL

### by

## Jon Sharpe

A SIGNET BOOK

SIGNET
Published by New American Library, a division of
Penguin Putnam Inc., 375 Hudson Street,
New York, New York 10014, U.S.A.
Penguin Books Ltd, 27 Wrights Lane,
London W8 5TZ, England
Penguin Books Australia Ltd, Ringwood,
Victoria, Australia
Penguin Books Canada Ltd, 10 Alcorn Avenue,
Toronto, Ontario, Canada M4V 3B2
Penguin Books (N.Z.) Ltd, 182–190 Wairau Road,
Auckland 10, New Zealand

Penguin Books Ltd, Registered Offices:
Harmondsworth, Middlesex, England

First published by Signet, an imprint of New American Library,
a division of Penguin Putnam Inc.

First Printing, April 2001
10  9  8  7  6  5  4  3  2  1

The first chapter of this title originally appeared in *Missouri Mayhem*,
the two hundred thirty-third volume in this series.

Printed in the United States of America

# The Trailsman

Beginnings . . . they bend the tree and they mark the man. Skye Fargo was born when he was eighteen. Terror was his midwife, vengeance his first cry. Killing spawned Skye Fargo, ruthless, cold-blooded murder. Out of the acrid smoke of gunpowder still hanging in the air, he rose, cried out a promise never forgotten.

The Trailsman they began to call him all across the West: searcher, scout, hunter, the man who could see where others only looked, his skills for hire but not his soul, the man who lived each day to the fullest, yet trailed each tomorrow. Skye Fargo, the Trailsman, the seeker who could take the wildness of a land and the wanting of a woman and make them his own.

*West Texas, 1858—*
*The desert is cruel,*
*even to those born to it . . .*

# 1

Skye Fargo unknotted the red bandanna from around his neck and squeezed out what seemed to be a quart of sweat. Mopping his weathered face helped a little but did nothing to ease the effects of the intensely bright West Texas sun hammering down unmercifully on him. He prayed for a breeze to evaporate the sweat sticking his shirt to his muscular body like a second skin, but the cruel desert refused. Not even a hint of wind blew across the rolling landscape. Like the promise of shade given by the thorny mesquite trees lining the long-dry arroyos, such cooling relief was only a lingering lie.

His lake-blue eyes studied the horizon and saw nothing there but the constant silvery heat shimmering. He turned in the saddle to look at his back trail. The faithful Ovaro shifted its weight and whinnied in complaint.

"I know, I know," Fargo said, patting the horse on the neck. "It's too hot for both of us." He had left Fort Stockton before dawn, thinking to be well along the road to Fort Davis before the sun turned the desert into a griddle and anyone foolish enough to ride across it into a strip of frying bacon.

That had been his plan, but Fargo had not considered the dearth of shelter once on the road. He had passed an abandoned stagecoach way station a couple hours outside Fort Stockton, but it had hardly been dawn then and he had kept riding, thinking he would find another suitable place to hole up until the fierce heat died and the sun sank in the west. Travel at twilight was more dangerous, since sidewinders and other, bigger predators came out to hunt then, but Fargo got along just fine with them. Mutual respect went a long way in defining territory, and he was always careful not to intrude, especially if the land's occupant had twin fangs capable of injecting poison.

But the sun! He could not avoid it as he would a sinuous poisonous snake. Fargo could only hide from it, and he had passed up that chance because there had not been another building of any sort in view for hours.

The Ovaro nickered and shook its head. Fargo patted its neck again. It wanted water. He had some in a canvas desert bag, but it was for him. And maybe it wasn't going to be enough. Fargo's mouth turned cottony as he lost more and more bodily moisture to sweat. He eyed the desert bag, cool and damp and inviting, but if he drank now, he might find himself in serious need of water farther along the dusty road.

He reached into his pocket and pulled out a small, smooth stone. The man known far and wide as the Trailsman popped it into his mouth and began rolling it around until saliva began to flow. It wasn't much, but it could keep a man alive. Fargo knew it had kept many an Apache alive in temperatures worse than he was enduring now.

Fargo considered giving his pony its head and seeing if it could sniff out the water that eluded him. The Apaches traveled this land constantly and knew every watering hole, as the Comanches had before them. The Comanches were gone, for the most part, but the Apaches, refusing to stay on their reservations, presented another threat in an already dangerous land.

Fargo snorted, mopped his forehead and fastened the bandanna back around his neck again before riding on slowly. Anything the Apaches could do, Fargo could also. He had proved that time and time again.

Right now he wanted nothing more than a tall arroyo embankment casting enough shade for both him and the Ovaro. Fargo knew better than to wish for an icy glass of lemonade. Such thoughts would only distract him from the serious business of staying alive.

"Got to be a spot for us to rest," Fargo said, judging the angle of the sun was working against him. The hot sun beat down directly at the top of his floppy-brimmed black felt hat, meaning it was noon.

He was in no particular hurry, other than to get out of the punishing sun for a spell. Fargo had scouted a bit out of Fort Stockton on a steady drift toward the west. Considering how punishing the sun was, he knew he should have headed northwest from Fort Stockton rather than west. Get to the Rockies and find a cool, clear running stream on some mountainside. Farther north and west he could lose himself for the entire summer in the Bitterroots. Montana and Idaho were mighty pretty this time of year.

"There it is," he said to his horse, tugging the reins a little to get the Ovaro headed in the right direction. A large ravine had been savagely cut by spring runoff months earlier, leaving a high bank. Not much shadow offered shelter this near noon, but in a half hour he would have a fine spot to nod off and wait for cooler temperatures.

The horse saw nothing to interest it but took little persuading to go where its rider insisted. The Ovaro was well trained and did whatever crazy thing Fargo demanded of it, even riding in the scorching midday summer desert heat.

Barely had he eased down the steep, sandy slope when Fargo reined back hard and canted his head to one side, listening for the faint sound of gunfire ahead. For a moment Fargo thought he had heard a mirage, if that was possible. If a man could see what wasn't there, why not hear a ghost gunfight?

The echoes convinced him he was not hallucinating. The gunshots were real. He heaved a sigh, checked the Colt riding at his hip and then the Henry rifle in its saddle sheath. He put his heels to the Ovaro's flanks and got the horse walking faster. To gallop in heat like this would kill the poor animal within a hundred yards.

Riding up the arroyo brought him to a road crossing it at a crazy angle. The spring runoff had cut through the road and made for dangerous passage then and difficult now, thanks to the loose gravel and sand on the ravine floor.

Fresh tracks showed Fargo that at least three wagons had passed within the hour. The sound of nearby gunshots carried an urgency, doubled by the war whoops of Apaches. Some settler had blundered off the main road Fargo had been following and gotten into big trouble with marauding Indians.

His work at Fort Stockton had included hunting for a band of Mescalero Apaches, but he had never been successful, always finding day-old spoor. Captain Murchison, the fort commandant, had figured the Apaches had finally left the region, heading west to cross the Rio Grande and find sanctuary in Mexico. By pure bad luck the settlers might have crossed paths with the Apaches.

The sharp scent of burning wood came to Fargo, borne on a hot wind blowing directly from the west. He gave the Ovaro its head, not wanting to push the horse beyond its limits. There might not be much he could do if the wagon train found itself attacked by fifty Indians— not much more than to reverse his course and return to Fort Stockton for a cavalry detachment. If he had to follow such an unpleasant path, leaving men and women to their fate, he wanted a strong horse able to carry him fast.

But Fargo doubted he would do anything like that, unless all the settlers were dead and all hope was gone. Saving them meant more than capturing the Indian renegades. Turning tail was not the way Fargo figured to rescue them. His hand brushed the solid butt of his Colt and then he reached level ground.

A quarter mile off, one wagon had broken down, leaving it easy prey for the Mescaleros. They had set fire to the wagon, driving the occupants toward the remaining two wagons. From the bodies on the ground, Fargo knew they had not gotten far before being cut down.

Whoops and rifle fire told him some resistance was being put up by the other two wagons. They tried to keep moving in spite of being under attack. This diverted the attention of at least one in the wagon from the serious job of shooting back at the Apaches.

"No," Fargo groaned when he saw the lead wagon had reached a fatal decision. Rather than park close to the other wagon so they could guard each other's backs and fight more effectively, the driver insanely was trying to outrun Indians on horseback.

He paid for this arrogance—or stupidity—quickly. The Indians swarmed around the fleeing wagon and killed the driver and the occupants within a minute, then set to stealing the mules pulling the wagon and looting the contents. Fargo turned his attention to saving the occupants of the remaining wagon. They had wisely stopped so all of them could fight off the circling Apaches, making it harder for the half dozen Indians to lift their scalps and steal their belongings.

Fargo unlimbered the Henry and brought it to his shoulder. The range was greater than he liked, but he was an expert marksman. His Ovaro stood stock still while he aimed and squeezed off the first round. The report caused the horse to shift a mite, then Fargo got a second shot off. Both found their targets. The first knocked an Apache off his horse, and the second winged one Fargo took to be the war leader.

His unexpected attack caused the Apaches to break off and come for him. As they turned their backs on the settlers, they found themselves being cut down from the rear. Fargo put a few more rounds into the air but found it harder to hit his targets. The Apaches' horses reared and bucked, and the warriors began riding low to avoid his fire.

Fargo fell into a steady rhythm of aim, squeeze, fire. He methodically sent leaden death winging toward the Indians until the Henry's tubular magazine came up empty. Replacing the rifle in its sheath, Fargo saw that more drastic action was needed if he wanted to save the settlers. The Apaches were not breaking off and running, as he had expected when he began taking potshots at them.

Drawing his Colt, he took a deep breath to settle himself. For good measure, he whipped out his Arkansas toothpick and waved it above his head so the blade caught the sunlight and reflected the death he sought to inflict.

"Hi-yaaa!" Fargo screeched at the top of his lungs.

5

Knife waving in one hand and pistol in the other, he guided his horse using only his knees. The Ovaro charged straight into the center of the tight knot of Apaches, trying to decide what to do, who to attack, how to do it.

Fargo got off three rounds from his six-shooter before the Indians broke and ran. They galloped hellbent for leather, him on their heels until it was obvious they were not going to regroup and attack again. Fargo stopped the frantic run and pulled the horse to a halt, kicking up dust as it dug in its heels.

He resheathed his Arkansas toothpick and shoved his six-gun into its holster before riding slowly toward the wagon. To be sure they didn't mistake him for a road agent come to rob them after the Apaches finished their attack, Fargo held his hands up over his head.

"Hello, are you all right?" he called. "The Apaches hightailed it. You're safe now."

Fargo expected a response. A heartfelt thanks, an angry growl or even a bullet intended to keep him at bay. Coldness knotted in his gut when he neared the wagon and no one responded in any way. He feared he had arrived too late to save the settlers.

"Anyone left alive?" he asked.

"Help us, mister," came a voice cracking with strain. "They done shot my ma and pa. Real bad."

Fargo rode closer and peered into the back of the wagon. Under the flapping, torn canvas arch he saw a young man, perhaps out of his teens but probably not, kneeling next to a man and woman. Both were covered with blood—their own.

He started to dismount but stopped when he saw movement from the corner of his eye. His hand flashed to his six-shooter and whipped it out. He had the gun cocked and aimed before he got a good look at his target. She was about the prettiest woman he had ever seen. Older than the young man in the wagon, in her early twenties, she was tall, dark-haired and had piercing blue eyes. There was a wild look he attributed to her brush with death, but it made her seem exotic, alive, and more vibrant than other women.

6

"A good thing you stopped, mister," she said. "He would have shot you." She pointed at a boy about ready to shave standing at her side. He held a Greener goose gun in shaking hands.

"Doubt it," Fargo said, dismounting. "He didn't close the chamber properly."

"Joshua!" she said, exasperated. "You could have got us all killed!" She stamped her foot and looked lovelier than ever. Fargo had to smile.

"Don't be too hard on him, ma'am," he said. "Truth is, bluffing sometimes works better than gunplay. I don't think I winged any of the Apaches after my first couple shots, but firing in their direction was a good use of the ammunition. Joshua here might have helped just poking that shotgun out and showing them he had it."

"You saved us, mister," Joshua said, coming over. He held the long-barreled shotgun as if he had never seen it before. "Can you show me what's wrong?"

"You got another shotgun around?" Fargo asked, taking the goose gun from him and prying loose the shell jammed into the chamber. "This is the wrong size for this gun."

"Oh," was all Joshua said.

"Help them," came the plea from within the wagon. "They are both hurt bad."

"That's my other brother, Abel," the young woman said. "I'm Rachel Cleary."

"Pleased to make your acquaintance," Fargo said, touching the brim of his battered hat. "You'd better see to your folks. I'll check the other wagons, just to be sure." He doubted anyone had survived in either of the other wagons. The one that had broken down had received the brunt of the Apache attack, and the driver who had tried to outrun horse-mounted Apaches with a mule team was obviously dead. Fargo saw him dangling over the edge of the driver's box.

"I'll come with you," Joshua said.

"If you want," Fargo said, "but you can be more use here. Help your brother and sister."

"We're doing what we can," Abel said sourly. "There's nothing he can do but mess up more."

7

"Tend the team," Fargo told the younger boy. "Get them ready for the trip back to Fort Stockton. That is where you set out from, isn't it?"

Joshua's head bobbed as if it were on a spring.

"But we're going to the town of La Limpia outside Fort Davis," Rachel complained. She poked her head out of the wagon. Her blouse was bloodstained now, as were her hands.

"If I'm any judge, Fargo said, "your folks need a real doctor," Fort Stockton is closer."

Fargo retrieved a half dozen mules from the second wagon, but they were the only living things he found. The Apaches had shown their usual viciously efficient style of fighting and left everyone other than the Cleary family dead. Poking through the few remaining items in the back of the wagons showed nothing worth loading. Fargo returned with the mules and hitched them in front of the Cleary team.

"I can't drive this many mules," Abel said. Everything he did showed how he wanted rid of Skye Fargo. Fargo thought the young man might feel a tad guilty about the way his folks had been wounded while he had come through the attack without so much as a scratch. As the oldest of the menfolk left unwounded in the Cleary family, Abel was trying to take over.

That wasn't too smart. Fargo had spent his entire life on the frontier and knew how to stay alive. Abel and the rest of his family were obvious greenhorns blundering around and lucky not to have died with the rest.

"Do you have a bullwhip?" Fargo asked. Joshua handed him the fifteen-foot whip. Fargo unrolled it, then snapped it in the air. "Toss a rock, will you, Joshua?"

When the boy did, Fargo cracked the whip and sent the rock sailing like a bullet.

"Do that right over a mule's ear and you can get him moving mighty fast," Fargo said. "I'm not an expert mule skinner, but I'm better than you."

"I—" Abel began.

"Thank you, sir," Rachel cut in. "We accept your help." She turned and angrily whispered to her brother. Abel jerked away and went back into the wagon.

"You've all been through more'n you expected," Fargo said. "Don't be too hard on him. But I can get you back to Fort Stockton faster than you can move on your own."

Rachel's bright blue eyes fixed on him as she wrestled with the decision. The slow smile that came to her lips was a little sad, as if she didn't like surrendering her family to a stranger either, but also happy that he had come by.

"My name's Fargo, Skye Fargo," he introduced. "Excuse my lack of manners, but . . ."

"But we've *all* been through more'n we expected," Rachel said, this time flashing him a genuine smile. She reached out and laid her hand on his for a fleeting moment, then turned and climbed into the wagon. She sat in the driver's box and stared down at him. "Well?" she asked. "When do we get rolling?"

It took the better part of three days before Fort Stockton came into view, set in the bowl of surrounding hills covered with grama grass and mesquites. Fargo had pushed as hard as he dared, but the wounded man and woman were in no condition to survive being bounced roughly around in the rear of the wagon. He had even argued hard with Abel over the liberal use of water and food. Returning had used more than a week's supplies, but it had kept them strong and their parents alive.

"I'm heading straight for the fort," Fargo said. "The post doctor is decent enough and has seen his share of bullet and arrow wounds."

"If he is the closest, Skye," Rachel said, a worried look on her face. "Mama is much stronger, but I am worried about Papa. He is drifting in and out of consciousness."

"That's a good sign," Fargo said. "It's better than him being in a coma. It shows he is fighting to stay alive. Out here, willpower is more important than about anything else."

"I suppose," she said, looking morose. Fargo had talked to her during the long hours of painstakingly slow travel and realized how forceful a personality her father

**9**

must have to drag the family from a comfortable life running a feed store in St. Louis to the frontier. Her father was a pioneer, a risk taker, and the others in the family weren't quite cut from the same cloth.

Rachel had a core of steel under the soft skin and behind the even softer words, but Fargo saw she preferred the civilized society of St. Louis to the dubious freedom and definite danger of West Texas.

Fargo cracked the bullwhip and got the team pulling toward the Fort Stockton gates. The sentry on duty recognized him and waved.

"Hey, Fargo, what'd you find out there? Any more like her left for me?" The private had eyes only for Rachel. Fargo saw how she blushed at the crude compliment. He also saw how she looked at him sideways, as if finding it acceptable enough that the guard thought he had returned with her as his woman.

"Go fetch Doc Martin," Fargo told Joshua. "That building straight ahead."

"Yes, sir," Joshua said, hitting the ground running. He stumbled and kept moving. Dr. Martin came from his surgery, followed by two soldiers, to see about the wounded Fargo was bringing in.

"Some things never change, do they, Fargo?" grumbled the doctor. "I thought I got rid of you hauling in so many injured for me to work on, but nope, you go trotting off and aren't gone a week when you bring more work for me."

"Don't go cutting off parts that don't need cutting, Doc," Fargo joked. He saw Rachel turn pale at such joshing. "Just get those folks patched up so they can be on their way again quick."

"Whatever you say, Fargo, but you owe me a drink for this. Two!"

"Consider it done," Fargo said, "*after* you finish working on them." He was still joking, but Rachel turned even paler.

"Come on," he told the young woman. "Let's go report to the fort commander. Captain Murchinson is a bit hidebound but a good man."

Fargo was aware of the looks they got as they crossed

the parade ground, heading for the commander's office. The men at Fort Stockton seldom saw any woman other than the soiled doves in town, a half mile off. And none of the women in these parts could hold a candle to Rachel's beauty.

"What brings you back?" Captain Murchison asked, pushing a pile of papers away when he saw Fargo and Rachel in front of his desk. The officer gave Rachel the once-over and then seemed to dismiss her.

Fargo gave a concise report about the Apache attack and ended by asking, "You want me to lead the patrol out after them?"

"Fargo, that must be the band of Mescaleros we already chased off. You think they were heading west, into Fort Davis territory?"

"They were," Fargo said.

"Then they aren't my concern anymore. Let them go. Let the commander at Fort Davis worry over them."

"You mean they're going to get away with killing all those people?" cried Rachel. "And my parents! They're badly injured. You can't just let the Indians—"

"Miss, I can and I will. My troops are on a short fuse right now. Pay has been scarce and the hours are getting longer. I've had fully one in ten of my men desert, making it even harder for those who are left. So, yes, I will let this band go."

"Even if Sharp Knife is leading them?" asked Fargo.

"As pleasing as that would be to me personally and as good as it would look on my official record, yes, even if Sharp Knife himself is leading them. Fargo, you know how hard it is here. I'd have to send half my men on a month-long patrol if that *is* Sharp Knife, and most of them might not return."

"So you'll let this Sharp Knife person kill and burn and pillage?" Rachel was outraged.

"Be glad you weren't among his victims, miss." Captain Murchison pointedly returned to his paperwork, dismissing them.

Rachel Cleary stamped her foot, spun, and flounced from the office. Fargo followed but did nothing to stop her as she hurried across the parade ground, returning to Dr. Martin's surgery. He had reported the attack to the responsible officer. He didn't like Murchison's answer any better than Rachel did, but Fargo understood it.

He *hated* it, but he understood it. From the point of view of the captain, it was both logical and guaranteed the safety of his soldiers.

Fargo set off to tend to his Ovaro and get back on the road for Fort Davis. Or maybe this time he would head north. The ferocious desert heat had a way of wearing down a man. Even the Trailsman.

# 2

Fargo disliked leaving Rachel and her two brothers stranded, but Fort Stockton was a better place for them and their parents than the middle of the desert.

And the Cleary family had not even reached the real desert when the Apache band had attacked them. They were still in the knee-high sere grass region, brown and deadly because of the lack of rain this year. Normally this part of Texas would have afforded a measure of grass for grazing and even water for travelers, but the dry winter and even drier spring had killed the land. The desert—the real desert—started farther west.

Fargo took some satisfaction in the Cleary family being safe and secure, even as he lamented the loss of the other two wagons filled with hopeful greenhorns who thought it would be an easy drive getting to Fort Davis in the middle of summer.

He stepped into the hot sun and wiped his forehead. From the way his forehead wrinkled from the heat, he might be forming arroyos all across his face. Fargo began to question his own reasons for heading toward the West Texas fort. In the desert he had imagined lovely, beguiling visions of snowcapped Montana mountains and lush Wyoming meadows and even Colorado peaks surging up to meet the brilliant, cloudless blue sky. Fargo looked westward and then north. From the middle of the fort's parade grounds he couldn't tell much difference. That would come only after a week or two of riding.

"Colorado or Fort Davis?" he wondered. He had headed for the isolated Texas fort because of rumors that the commander needed a good scout and had problems finding one willing to endure the heat and hardship. Captain Murchison had no further use for him at Fort Stockton because he could not even pay the regular Army troopers. Besides, with Apache activity picking up, the Trailsman's unique talents might be put to good use. Sharp Knife had definitely headed westward toward Fort Davis, possibly thinking to cross the Rio Grande into Mexico.

Fargo hated to admit it even to himself, but he needed a challenge to keep his talents sharp and his mind alert. Tracking Apache raiders would bring him back to life after dull garrison duty and occasional scouts away from Fort Stockton.

"I'm going stale," he said, "but I can find work in Colorado, and if I don't, a summer spent hunting and fishing in the high country wouldn't do me any harm."

Decision made, Fargo headed for the stables to retrieve his Ovaro. He hoped that fort sutler had enough supplies available for him to buy for his new, longer trip. It was dry and dusty riding west. Heading north would be even worse until after he passed Cap Rock country around Amarillo. Before he got to the far side of the dusty parade ground, he heard someone calling his name.

"Fargo, hey, Skye Fargo, wait up!" A bandy-legged man with a big, drooping handlebar mustache came running up. A star shone on his chest.

"Didn't expect to see you again, Marshal," Fargo greeted. Ethan Goldman was federal marshal for the region and often locked horns with Murchison over how to keep the peace. Fargo had developed a liking for the short, sturdy man and his intense beliefs about strict law enforcement. This might be another reason Murchison so easily let Fargo ride off from Fort Stockton.

"You brought in a family of settlers, I heard."

"News travels fast," Fargo allowed.

"You seein' them back on the trail? You scoutin' for 'em?" Goldman cocked his head to one side and peered at Fargo. One of the marshal's eyes had gone milky, but the other was sharp and clear.

"The father and mother were shot up pretty bad.

Reckon it'll take them a spell to get back on their feet, and when they do, who knows what they will decide? They came from St. Louis." Fargo shrugged. "Might decide St. Louis looks better than a piece of the Chihuahua Desert."

"That's not even desert out where you found 'em," Goldman said, looking miffed that Fargo was crediting the land with being more deadly than it really was. "Wait till they see *real* desert."

"You were deputy over in Tucson, weren't you?"

"I got tales of the Sonoran Desert that'd curl your hair. Never mind that. I got a hot trail to follow, and it's not injuns. You want a piece of the reward for Frederickson?"

"Who's that?"

"Who's that!" shouted Goldman, getting excited and jumping about as if he were a flea dropped onto a hot griddle. "Why, Big Red Frederickson is about the biggest, meanest, ugliest outlaw this side of the Mississippi. He's been running guns and doing even worse. Rumor has it he's sellin' firewater to the Apaches along with new rifles and plenty of ammo. That's a bad mix no matter how you cut it."

"You know where he is?"

"North of Fort Stockton, in the hills."

"If you can call those lumps hills," Fargo said, thinking about Colorado, where real mountains started at fourteen thousand feet.

"Won't argue that with you, Fargo. I spent a year or more in Las Animas. But do you want to pass up a hunnerd-dollar reward?"

Fargo found himself considering the marshal's offer. The pay he had received from Captain Murchison was barely a quarter that for a month's scouting, and he had considered himself lucky to get one red cent.

"I can see you're thinkin' on it. Like, what if ole Ethan's off his bean or that was a bum rumor? I'll put you on my payroll as a deputy for a week. We find Frederickson, fine. If not, then you wasted a week but earned a decent salary."

"How decent?" Fargo found himself dickering over

nickels and dimes, probably because that was what Goldman expected of him. Fargo was never quite sure when he made up his mind to ride along with the banty rooster of a lawman, but the ten dollars the marshal promised for the week was a big inducement.

And in the back of Fargo's mind was the notion he could spend the week tracking Frederickson, then swing back past Fort Stockton and see how Rachel and her family were getting along. Seeing such a pretty, frisky filly would always be a treat.

"So?" demanded Marshal Goldman. "What do ya make of the tracks?"

Fargo got on hands and knees and studied the jumble of hoofprints. The day before, they had found an abandoned campsite Goldman assured him had belonged to Big Red Frederickson. With no evidence to the contrary, Fargo had accepted the lawman's word and they had tracked two riders north toward Cap Rock country. But the trail was shifting, heading away from Palo Duro Canyon and veering due west. If Frederickson—or whomever they were tracking—kept going in that direction, he'd end up in Magoffinsville, Texas, just across the Mexican border from El Paso del Norte.

"Can't say they know we're on their trail, but it looks like the riders are hightailing it away from their original destination. What's to the west of here?"

Goldman shrugged. "Go far enough, you wind up in the Guadalupe Mountains. Word has it Sharp Knife and his renegades are holed up there. Do you think Frederickson is selling guns to Sharp Knife?"

"If he is, he's not selling many," Fargo said. "Four horses went on from here. The two we followed from the camp joined up with two others who'd waited for a few hours. But how many rifles can four saddle horses carry?"

"Not many," admitted Goldman. "We don't have to catch him peddlin' guns, though. Just catch him. He's got an inch of wanted posters on his head. You ought to see 'em on my desk back in town."

Fargo nodded but barely heard the lawman. He

**16**

walked down a steep slope and followed the four horses to a narrow trail at the foot of the ridge they had followed. The hills were tall enough to block from view anyone traveling more than a mile or two away, but big enough to catch and trap the stifling summer heat. Fargo saw no reason for the riders to leave the ridge, with its hint of cooling breeze, to suffocate in the valley created by the meandering hills.

"That's the reason," he said, pointing.

"What is it?" Goldman squinted, but his one good eye missed what to the Trailsman was an obvious track.

"Wagons. Two of them. The riders joined up with the wagons and took off in that direction." Fargo pointed toward the distant, invisible Guadalupe Range.

"Hot damn," cried Goldman. "Frederickson's goin' to meet up with Sharp Knife. I knew it!"

"How long are you willing to chase after them?" Fargo asked.

"To the ends of the earth, that's how far," Goldman declared.

"You think the pair of us can take this gang? Four riders, maybe that many more men in the wagons."

"Two against eight? Why, many's the time over in Tucson—you knew I was a deputy in Tucson?—I'd go up against twice that many. I'm here, 'live and kickin'.'" Goldman grinned broadly. "I'm not only here, I'm ridin' with the best danged frontiersman what ever lived!"

Fargo brushed aside such compliments quickly. It flattered him, but he had to be realistic. Gunrunners were suspicious folks. That kept them alive and prospering in their deadly trade. Even if Frederickson had shipped a few cases of whiskey and his gang drank heavily, Fargo was not sure the two of them could take on eight outlaws.

And, he had to admit, he might be wrong about the number. There could be a half dozen more men riding in the wagons. That meant more ways to divvy the illegal proceeds from selling the rifles, but it also guaranteed that Sharp Knife and other Apache war chiefs would not simply kill the gunrunners and steal the rifles.

"They're moving slow," Fargo said, walking along the

tracks left by the two wagons. "See how deep the wheels cut, even in this sun-baked ground?"

"Likely to be guns and ammo rather than whiskey," Goldman said, coming to the same conclusion Fargo already had.

Fargo walked a few hundred yards farther, then stopped. He held up his hand and motioned the marshal to silence. The wagons had been pulling along at a steady clip, but here they had slowed. He could tell from the way one wagon wheel wobbled. Dropping the Ovaro's reins, Fargo went ahead on foot, straining to hear the slightest sound.

The drone of insects on the windless air was all he heard until he went another hundred yards. Then he smelled horses. Fargo turned slowly, homing in on the smell. It had to be drifting down the valley from ahead. Decided on this, he advanced and finally heard mules braying.

Fargo waved to Goldman, signaling the lawman to approach quietly. While the marshal was not as good as Fargo, he made his way up the deep gulch as silent as a puff of wind.

"What you find?" Goldman asked in a husky whisper. The tips of his mustache twitched, and he rested his hand on the six-gun holstered at his hip.

"Hear it?"

Ethan Goldman frowned, concentration written in every line in his face. Then he brightened. "I surely do, Fargo. Mules. It's got to be Frederickson!"

"Might be, if we've really been following him and not some legitimate businessman."

"Legit? Out here in the middle of nowhere?" Goldman looked as if he was going to spit, but his mouth was too dry for that.

Fargo saw that the lawman had a point. Even if they weren't trailing Big Red Frederickson, something illegal was going on. No one in their right mind ventured out in such searing heat to sell yard goods or ten-penny nails.

"What do you want to do, Fargo?" Goldman asked, pursing his lips and looking anxiously up the valley.

"First thing I want to do is get a peek at what lies

around the bend." Fargo pointed ahead to the heat haze–shrouded twist in the land. Their quarry wasn't far past the turn.

"Might be a good idea to wait for twilight," Goldman said. "I'm champin' at the bit to go do some arrestin', but we might stand a better chance with dusk hidin' our approach."

"I'll see what I can and report back," Fargo said. As he left he smiled. He sounded as if he were still working for Captain Murchison. Then he settled down and advanced carefully, avoiding patches of prickly pear cactus and clumps of dry grass that might crackle under his boots and betray him. Following the opposite side of the ridge until he judged he was near their quarry's camp, he started up the slope and then dropped to his belly. Hot rocks and burning sand seared his underside. How a sidewinder survived in this land was beyond Fargo's comprehension. Staying low, he slipped forward and then had a view down into the camp a couple dozen yards away.

He counted men and finished when he came to ten. Then he saw the eleventh man coming from behind a clump of creosote bush. Fargo had never seen Big Red Frederickson before, nor had he read the description on the wanted poster, but he knew this was their man. He was tall, inches taller than Fargo, and had a shock of flame-red hair that was almost painful to look at. Although bulky, Frederickson seemed to drift like a feather, light on his feet. Fargo decided the outlaw would probably have a quick draw from the way he moved.

Two wagons had been pulled up, but their teams were still hitched. Fargo took that to mean the buyers for the merchandise hidden under tarps over the wagon beds would be along soon. If he and Goldman wanted to arrest Frederickson, they'd have to move fast. Against eleven men it was difficult. Against more joining the gunrunners, it would be impossible.

Fargo returned to where Goldman was waiting impatiently and explained the situation.

"Arresting them without gunplay isn't going to happen," Fargo told the lawman. "I can't see them throwing up their hands and surrendering without a fight. There's too many of them. Even if we had a full posse backing us up, Frederickson and his men would shoot it out."

"Strange how havin' a dozen guns to defend you gives you a false sense of security," Goldman said. He smiled after a few more seconds. "Distract them. Go on up the valley and set fire to some brush or cause a ruckus. That will pull some of them away from the wagons. When they go, I'll arrest Frederickson. I want them others so bad I can taste it, but arrestin' him will be good enough for now."

"Cut off the head and the snake dies?"

"Not till sundown," Goldman said, repeating an old wives' tale that Fargo had never found to be true. "We'll have to risk this snake stayin' dangerous after we lop off its head."

"Let's get to taking the head back to Fort Stockton," Fargo said, slipping his Henry from its sheath. "It's too dangerous setting a fire with the grasslands this dry. I'll kick up a fuss and see how many of them come to investigate."

"That'll do me," Goldman said optimistically. "If Frederickson goes to poke around, you arrest him. Otherwise, I'll take him."

They split, Fargo knowing how dangerous this was. They were outnumbered almost six to one. Surprise was their best weapon. Then it had to be speed. If the marshal did his job right, the rest of the gunrunners might not notice their boss had been grabbed from under their noses. That could give them enough time to put a few miles between them and the outlaws.

First, Fargo had to decoy as many of the gunrunners as possible. He crossed over the ridge a hundred yards away from the wagons. Through the heat haze he saw the men lounging under the wagons, hunting for any shade they could find. It bothered him that they didn't know what was in the wagons, but Marshal Goldman had positively identified Red Frederickson. The man was wanted, and that was good enough for Fargo.

He lifted the Henry to his shoulder and aimed carefully. The round ricocheted off a metal-rimmed wagon wheel and spooked the otherwise staid mules. When they strained against their harnesses, the wagons moved and scared the men hiding from the sun underneath.

The startled outlaws milled around for a moment, not sure what was going on. Fargo added a few more rounds that sank into the wooden sides of the wagon to get the mules moving in his direction. Frederickson yelled orders, and eight outlaws whipped out six-shooters and grabbed for their rifles before starting in his direction.

It was time for Fargo to make himself scarce. He had lured them away, and the rest was up to Ethan Goldman.

Halfway up the hill, making use of what vegetation he could find to hide his retreat, Fargo looked back in the direction of the two rifle-laden wagons and stopped. He stood upright and waved, yelling a warning to Goldman at the top of his lungs.

The marshal had timed his approach perfectly, coming up behind Frederickson when the outlaw least expected it. Goldman even had the towering red-haired gunrunner moving back up the hill to where they could whisk him away.

Neither of them had counted on Frederickson's clients showing up at this precise moment.

An Apache war chief and a half dozen warriors rode up and saw what was happening.

Ethan Goldman didn't have a chance. The chief and all six of his braves fired point-blank at the lawman. Fargo watched in shocked wonder as Goldman danced about every time a new bullet ripped through his body. He had died fast, but the Apache fusillade refused to let him fall. Like a marionette, the marshal twisted and jerked and finally, his bones broken by the myriad bullets, he fell to the ground.

Then Fargo realized his own danger. He had yelled the warning to the marshal, hoping the lawman could get away. Goldman had died and Fargo had attracted the Apaches' attention to himself.

He lit out, running hard, but Fargo knew he would lose the race—the race to stay alive.

# 3

Fargo's boots slid from under him when he hit a patch of loose gravel. He sat down hard, sliding along the far slope of the hill away from the gunrunners. Behind, he heard Apache war whoops and the loud curses from Frederickson's men as they sought out anyone with Goldman. Fargo didn't see any of them yet but knew they had to be climbing the far side of the hill, hot on his trail.

He slid to the bottom of the slope, got his feet under him, and ran for the horses. Before he reached the spot where he and Goldman had tethered their horses, a bullet sang through the air just above his head. Then came another and another, but these were far off target. The first had been a lucky shot, nothing more. Fargo knew relying on luck much longer would mean his death. Whatever he did now had to be smart and quick—and right.

Whirling around when he reached the two horses, he scanned the ridge and saw a pair of men lumbering along the top. Fargo lifted his Henry, aimed, and fired. The first shot brought down one man. The second missed entirely but drove the other outlaw to cover. As Fargo went to mount his horse, he saw something that sent a chill up his spine.

Coming around the hill, cutting off his retreat down the valley, were a half dozen Apaches. Leading them rode their war chief, all decked out in war paint. Fargo's eyes locked with the Apache chief's for a moment. He had never been close enough to see Sharp Knife's face before, but he knew this had to be the warrior terrorizing West Texas. An ugly wound showed where Fargo had creased the chief earlier during his attack on the Cleary wagon.

Fargo swung into the saddle of Goldman's mount and put his heels to the horse's flanks. As he rode past his Ovaro, he bent low and scooped up the reins. The jerk as the reins came free of the sagebrush where he had tethered the horse almost unseated him. Fargo hung on grimly, frightening his horse and brutally yanking on the bridle.

There was no way around such harshness. He had to get the horse to a full gallop. He didn't want to leave the Ovaro behind, and there wasn't time to be gentle, not unless he wanted to leave his own scalp dangling from Sharp Knife's belt. The Apache chief and his braves were galloping toward him and would overtake him in a few minutes.

Fargo wished he could switch horses and ride his own but knew this was for the best. Ethan Goldman had no need for a horse any longer, and Fargo did. He rode the animal into the ground. The mare began to stumble and tire after two miles of hard galloping. Lather flecked the animal's sides, its eyes went wide from exertion, and the harsh gasping and heaving flanks told him the horse couldn't maintain the pace much longer.

He pushed the horse for another hundred yards before it died under him. The gallant horse collapsed, but Fargo was ready. He hit the ground, stumbled and fell, rolled and came to his feet, hanging onto the reins of his own horse. As the Ovaro trotted past, he swung into the familiar saddle.

Looking back, he saw he had outraced Sharp Knife. For the moment. The Apaches had wisely decided not to kill their horses coming after him, but he knew they were behind him, sniffing out his tracks like bloodhounds. If Big Red Frederickson did not goad them into finding and killing him, Sharp Knife would take it into his head to do so on his own. Their transfer of stolen goods for the rifles had been interrupted by a federal marshal. Both Frederickson and the Apache war chief would want to keep their dealings as quiet as possible.

The marshal was dead. All they needed to do to keep word of the illicit gunrunning from reaching other ears was to kill Skye Fargo.

Fargo was not certain Captain Murchison would send a patrol out, but with the town of Fort Stockton's federal marshal dead, he might not have a choice. Whatever Sharp Knife was up to—and it didn't look as if the Apache was in any hurry to cross the Rio Grande— having a cavalry unit dogging his steps would pose a problem. And Frederickson would be even less anxious to have the U.S. Army on patrol hunting for him. Murchison might take it into his head to collect the reward and possibly pay some of his men. A hundred dollars went a ways toward the back wages owed most of the men on his post.

All this flashed through Fargo's mind, and then he settled down to escape. The Ovaro was tired but able to keep up a brisk pace. Fargo changed gait often, trotting the horse, then walking it. He wished he could dismount and walk alongside it, but some sixth sense told him the Apaches were getting closer.

He hoped only Sharp Knife's braves were after him. If Frederickson sent any of his men, Fargo could never elude them because of their overwhelming numbers.

"I wanted a challenge," Fargo mocked himself. "Getting away from a band of Mescalero Apaches certainly is that—and more." Fargo chided himself for getting what he had wished for. He left the valley where he had ridden Goldman's horse into the ground and cut up a narrow ravine, climbing steadily, protected by the deeply cut banks. As he reached the top of the hill, he looked back and saw how close the Apaches were to catching him.

He knew their horses had to be close to exhaustion, but the Apache ponies were as strong-hearted as their riders. Fargo knew he could take a few long-range shots, but that would only give away his position. He could never fight six braves, including Sharp Knife, and win unless he took them by surprise. Right now they were alert and ready for him to stop and shoot it out with them.

Fargo struggled to the top of the hill and went down the far side. Then he dismounted to give the Ovaro a rest. He drew his Arkansas toothpick and hacked at sage and creosote bush until he had a big ball. Using his lariat, he tied the bushes to the end, then weighed it down with a few stones expertly stuck into the rope's fiber.

"I hate to do this, but we've got miles more to go," Fargo said, patting the horse's neck. Then he mounted and looped the other end of his lariat around the saddle horn. Riding slowly, he checked his back trail. The bushes erased the imprints of the horse's hooves left in the dusty ground. A good tracker would spot the way the bushes cut even grooves and how a cleared swath was just the right width to cover a trail, but it would have to do for now.

Fargo hoped the setting sun would cause a wind to kick up. That would help hide his trail. He went down the valley parallel to the one where he had outridden the Apaches, doubling back in the direction of Frederickson's wagons. As he rode, the brush wore away, forcing Fargo to cut more. This gave the Ovaro another minute or two to rest and Fargo a chance to see if the Apaches were still ready to breathe down his neck.

In the twilight he could not tell where the Indians were. He heard nothing but the faint, mournful whine of wind kicking up over the dry land. This would cover his tracks even better than he had done, but not if the Apaches outguessed him. Fargo reined back and let his horse rest. He needed to think.

He needed to outthink the Apaches.

Doubling back the way he had might have thrown them off his trail, but he could not count on it. Sharp Knife would never believe a white man was foolish enough to go after Frederickson when a federal marshal had been gunned down, so that way might be Fargo's safest route. But following the gunrunners posed new problems. How could he be sure Sharp Knife's band wouldn't ride up behind him as he followed Frederickson?

How could he know where Frederickson intended to

go after selling the guns to the Apaches? Fargo realized he might find himself facing the outlaws as they retraced their path to the rendezvous point.

Stars began popping out in the black velvet sky. The moon wouldn't rise for another hour or two, giving Fargo a bit of time to escape—or to go after Frederickson. He vowed to bring Marshal Goldman's killers to justice, starting with the leader of the gunrunners. The Apaches had cut down the marshal, but they would not have been on the prairie if Frederickson had not offered them rifles and ammo.

"Frederickson will give Captain Murchison something worth going after," Fargo said softly. His sharp eyes scanned the ridges, looking for any telltale sign of Apaches coming after him. He saw nothing, but he knew this meant little. They were masters at warfare, although they seldom fought after dark because of the rattlesnakes that spooked them so.

While the Apaches disliked fighting after sundown, that didn't mean they would not. Fargo suspected the Mescaleros in Sharp Knife's band feared their leader more than any rattlesnake.

The Ovaro shifted nervously and whinnied. Fargo bent forward to soothe the horse, then without warning he found himself pitched headlong from the saddle. As he sailed through the air, he twisted and landed hard on his back, his fingers curling around the butt of his six-shooter.

Looming above him was the silhouette of an Apache warrior. Fargo fired point-blank into the shadowy form and before the smoke cleared from the Colt's barrel, he was fighting for his life, pinned squarely under the brave's heavy body. His six-gun was knocked to one side, and Fargo grasped a brawny wrist trying to drive a knife into his throat.

Fargo twisted and thrashed around, trying to unseat the Apache. Nothing worked. The warrior wore him down, the knife inching toward Fargo's face. He tightened his grip on the Indian's wrist, trying to cut off circulation and force him to drop the blade, but Fargo's fingers started slipping.

With the knife tip only inches above him, the Apache suddenly sagged. Fargo heaved and threw the man off. He rolled to his knees and grabbed for his Arkansas toothpick, then relaxed. The wetness that had prevented him from getting a decent grip on the Apache's wrist had been blood—the Apache's. Fargo's shot had caught the warrior in the chest.

"Fighting a dead man," Fargo marveled. Although mortally wounded, the Apache had kept fighting and had almost taken Fargo to the grave with him. Fargo wiped the blood from his fingers and then retrieved his six-shooter. The report might have drawn others.

Fargo whistled, got the Ovaro trotting over to him, and swung into the saddle. The Apache had come up on him, and only the horse's skittishness had alerted him. Fargo had done what he had to—and would again when he came up against Sharp Knife himself.

But now the fight had to be left for another day. Let Big Red Frederickson and his gunrunners get away scot-free. Let Sharp Knife and his braves go back to the warpath with their new rifles. Fargo had to tell Murchison what had happened and alert everyone in Fort Stockton that their marshal was dead.

He hated turning tail and running like this, but staying alive counted for more now than foolish—and probably fatal—heroism. As Fargo headed back for Fort Stockton, he knew he had not seen the last of Frederickson and Sharp Knife.

Fargo would be there when they were brought to justice. He owed that to Ethan Goldman.

# 4

Tired from the long ride and dejected over his inability to save Marshal Goldman from the gunrunners and Apaches, Fargo rode back to Fort Stockton. He turned grim when he saw Captain Murchison inspecting the neat rows of troops standing at attention on the parade ground. Those men would be out in the field soon, on patrol after Frederickson and Sharp Knife. How many of them would die like Marshal Goldman? If Fargo had to guess, the answer would be "too many."

Murchison looked up and scowled when he saw Fargo. The officer finished his inspection, then went to the covered porch of his office and waited in the shade, seeing that Fargo did not bring good news.

"What is it, Fargo?" he asked brusquely. "I have to get a column ready for a patrol."

"Marshal Goldman's dead," Fargo said. He took no pleasure from Murchison's reaction. The captain's eyebrows arched, and he started to say something. His mouth opened, then closed, then opened again and now words came out.

Finally, Murchison croaked, "How? What happened?"

"A gunrunner named Big Red Frederickson," Fargo said. Then he added the name that Murchison did not want to hear. "And Sharp Knife. He was buying rifles from Frederickson."

"Damn," was all the captain said.

"Should I report to the marshal's office in town? They deserve to know they have to send for another federal marshal."

"The town marshal can handle local law enforcement

for a spell," Murchison said. The man's attention was a hundred miles away as he considered everything Fargo had told him. The world was coming apart around him, and he had too few soldiers to enforce the peace.

"The sheriff can help, too, if he's not spending all his time serving process." Fargo knew the lawmen got paid so poorly they had to take other jobs to make ends meet. Serving court orders paid better than arresting disorderly drunks or making sure dead animals did not litter the streets. It also kept the lawmen away from town, where they were most likely to be needed.

"Get into the office and show me on the map where this happened." Murchison fixed his gaze on Fargo. "I don't have money to hire you."

"I don't care," Fargo told him. "I'll lead the patrol for nothing. This is personal."

The Fort Stockton commander bellowed for his sergeants and got a shavetail lieutenant to lead twenty men into the field. He briefed them quickly, then said with some distaste, "Mr. Fargo will take you to the place where the gunrunners passed their contraband to the Apaches."

"What are your orders, sir?" asked the lieutenant, looking frightened at the prospect of going into the field. Fargo did not recognize the man and wondered if he had just transferred into the post. Probably. Even worse, the young lieutenant might be on his first foray against a real enemy.

"Take Frederickson into custody with as many of his men as possible. Stop Sharp Knife. Capture or destroy the rifles."

"Capturing them rifles would help us out a mite, sir," spoke up a sergeant who had seen a fair amount of skirmishing with both Apaches and Comanches. "We can use the weapons and the ammunition."

"Yes, of course," Murchison said, as if dismissing such a crazy notion.

The soldiers saluted and Murchison went back into his office, grumbling to himself. Fargo saw that the captain was risking almost a third of his command while remaining personally safe and secure behind the stockade walls.

"You going to scout for us, Fargo?" asked the sergeant.

"Looks like," Fargo agreed. He saw the lieutenant had no idea what was going on.

"Get the troops mounted, Sergeant," Fargo said, taking command. "I'll tell the lieutenant about the lay of the land and what we face."

The sergeant nodded, cast a quick contemptuous glance at the officer, then hurried off, yelling orders as he went. The soldiers jumped to, obeying their sergeant's commands.

"This is no cakewalk, Lieutenant," Fargo said. He went on to tell the officer everything he had seen and how he had barely escaped the Apaches.

"You're the one they call the Trailsman, aren't you?" the lieutenant said, a hint of awe in his voice. "And you say you had a time of it?"

"Outnumbered, outgunned, and not wanting to leave Marshal Goldman," Fargo said, cold rage building. "Sometimes you have to retreat so you can regroup and attack again."

"Like now, sir?" asked the lieutenant.

"Like now," Fargo answered.


"Ahead," Fargo said, pointing up the narrow valley where Goldman had been killed trying to arrest Big Red Frederickson. "You can see the deep ruts left by the wagons."

The lieutenant looked confused. "I don't see anything," he finally said. "Are you sure this is the place?"

"Ahead, and yes, I am sure," Fargo said irritably. "I doubt they stuck around waiting for us. The wagons rolled on up the valley, heading in the direction of Amarillo. They might have taken another road and headed somewhere else since they didn't double back on this trail."

"Sergeant," called the lieutenant, his voice a little shaky. "The scout says we're almost at the place where the gunrunners sold firearms to the Indians. Take your squad to the top of the ridge."

"It's not a good idea splitting such a small force," Fargo said. "Frederickson had almost a dozen men with him, and I saw almost that many more Apaches with Sharp Knife. That makes us about equal in firepower, or maybe outnumbered by one or two men."

"You said it yourself. There's no reason for them to stay here."

"I—" Fargo found himself talking to the lieutenant's back. The officer curtly ordered the sergeant to take the squad up the ridge and immediately signaled the remainder of the platoon to follow him. He wasn't even waiting for the sergeant to report back.

"If you're attacked, it'll take the sergeant too long to come to your aid if you rush in," Fargo said, trotting up alongside the officer. "Wait a few minutes. The men can use the rest. This heat is stifling."

"I thought you were a tough frontiersman," the lieutenant said. His face had sunburned and blistered in places, but he put up a stubborn front.

"Tough but not stupid," Fargo said. He saw right away he should have sweet-talked the lieutenant. All he had succeeded in doing was firming the young officer's resolve to bull ahead because it looked as if the man was not in command. Fargo considered knocking the lieutenant off his horse to delay the column's advance. Then it was too late.

The lieutenant let out a yelp of delight. "There's the marshal's body. By the back wagon."

Fargo rode up and went cold inside. The gunrunners had abandoned their wagons. He tried to remember how many outlaws had ridden in the rear of the wagons. Then he spotted a small rope corral farther up the valley they had followed, holding a dozen horses.

"Trap!" Fargo yelled.

Too late.

The tarps in the rear of both wagons flew off and the Apaches leaped up, using the rifles they had traded for against the cavalry. Three soldiers died in the first fusillade. The troopers with the lieutenant scattered rather than grouping to return fire. This spelled their deaths as the Apaches picked them off one by one.

Fargo pulled out his Henry and got off a few shots, missing every time because of the way his Ovaro bucked and tried to bolt and run. He fought to regain control as bullets whizzed past his head.

"Sergeant!" Fargo bellowed. He hoped the veteran trooper would get back down the slope from the ridge in time to save some of the troopers caught in the jaws of the Apache trap. Sharp Knife had left four warriors in hiding in the wagons. The rest of his band was mounted and charging back down the valley straight for the disoriented, frightened soldiers.

Fargo got his horse under control and tried to decide where he could put his rifle to the best use. The lieutenant was shouting orders left and right, but that only added to the confusion in the soldiers' ranks. A shot to take the lieutenant out of the battle might be the best thing he could do for the troopers, but Fargo wouldn't do that.

Especially when he spotted Sharp Knife among the Indians on horseback. This had become personal between him and the Apache chief. Fargo leveled his rifle, took careful aim, and squeezed off a shot.

"Missed!" he exclaimed. He had missed but not by much. One of the eagle feathers stuck in Sharp Knife's hair had a notch shot in it now. But Fargo had no chance for a second shot.

Sharp Knife rallied his braves from the rear of the wagons and got them to the rope corral, mounted and riding hellbent for leather away from the scene of the massacre. Fargo saw the reason. The sergeant had responded right away to the sounds of battle, and his squad had galloped back to the valley floor. Sharp Knife might not know how many reinforcements he faced.

Or . . .

"After them," screamed the lieutenant, picking himself up off the ground. His horse had been shot out from under him. He looked uninjured but was madder than a wet hen. "Sergeant, stop those red bastards!"

"No!" snapped Fargo. "Sharp Knife retreated too fast.

He probably has another trap set ahead, if you're fool enough to chase after him."

"Sergeant, who is in command?" The lieutenant came over and glared up at the sergeant. The sergeant looked from his commander to Fargo and then back.

"Sir, I went a tad deaf during the fight. Too much gunfire too close to my head. What was it you said?"

"It's too late to go after them," Fargo said, trying to detour the lieutenant's wrath away from the noncom. "We're tired from getting out here from the fort. Their horses were rested."

"I'll have your stripes for insubordination," the lieutenant cried. He spun and glared at Fargo. "I'd have you hanged, if I could. You led us into an ambush, and you call yourself a scout!"

"Sir, he warned you."

"Silence!" roared the lieutenant. "Someone, get me a horse."

"Don't go after Sharp Knife," Fargo warned. "You'll never see another sunrise if you do."

"I can't go after him," the lieutenant said, breathing hard. "I need to get the wounded men back to Fort Stockton. Sergeant, have the wounded and dead loaded into those wagons. We'll use them."

"How you intend to pull the wagons, Lieutenant? Saddle horses don't act too good harnessed to a wagon."

"Do it, do it, do it!" shrieked the lieutenant, losing control. He mounted a horse brought to him by a corporal and went off to supervise those taking care of the wounded.

"You did what you could, Fargo," the sergeant said when his commander was out of earshot. "The Apaches are sneaky bastards, and he walked into the trap with his eyes wide open."

"I don't care if he blames me," Fargo said "I'll do what I can to keep Murchison from taking your stripes. You're the only one out here with a speck of common sense."

"You do what you have to, Fargo," the sergeant said. "Don't worry none 'bout me. I been busted to private before. Twice, in fact. Third time's the charm."

"The cavalry needs men like you. Don't quit."

"Quit?" The sergeant laughed. "There's nothin' else I know. Besides, runnin' down the like of Sharp Knife is what I enjoy doin' most."

"Good luck," Fargo said, meaning it. The sergeant threw him a smart salute, then went to get his squad squared away before the lieutenant confused them too much.

Fargo rode away slowly, feeling as if he was deserting a friend in need. Still, the sergeant was right. He'd be promoted quickly again because Captain Murchison needed veteran soldiers more than he needed wet-behind-the-ears lieutenants getting his men killed.

When he reached the top of the ridge, he looked north. Sharp Knife had ridden that way, but Fargo had the feeling the Apache war chief's camp wouldn't be there. The Apaches had been ranging farther west—and much farther south, away from the dry prairie and into real desert near Fort Davis.

He turned the Ovaro's face and headed in the direction his gut dictated.

Five days. Fargo had trailed the Apache renegades for five days before he overtook them. He sat beside a broad waist-high patch of prickly pear cactus, hidden from sight of the solitary sentry at Sharp Knife's camp. The Indians had set up camp early to keep from traveling at night and finally had given Fargo the chance to square things away with Sharp Knife. The Apache war chief sat near the fire, roasting a rabbit shot an hour earlier, just at dusk.

The smell of cooking meat made Fargo's mouth water. He had run short of water, lived off jerky and nothing more during the chase. Now the cooking odors were torturing him. The only satisfaction Fargo had was that Sharp Knife had no idea anyone was within a hundred miles of him.

The sentry walked within ten feet of Fargo, oblivious to him. Fargo bided his time. During the chase he had thought hard what he wanted to accomplish. With a dozen braves around him, Sharp Knife thought he was invulnerable. As far as a frontal, all-out attack went, that was true. But a single man sneaking into camp and spiriting away the chief was not out of the question.

At least, Fargo hoped it was possible, because he was going to try.

This renegade had killed Ethan Goldman, slaughtered greenhorn settlers and severely wounded Rachel Cleary's parents, dealt with gunrunners, and then had lain in wait for the cavalry to investigate before killing them. He had to be brought to justice, and neither Captain Murchison nor his inexperienced lieutenant was likely to succeed.

The Trailsman would.

A little before midnight, the once-alert sentry settled down and nodded off to sleep. Fargo left his hiding place and silently walked into the middle of the Apache camp. The fires had burned to embers, and the Indians slept fitfully, making detection at any instant likely. Fargo kept moving, his gait uneven and as much like the rhythm of the cold, fitful desert wind as possible.

He stopped beside Sharp Knife and stared at the Apache war chief. The hard lines on the man's face did not soften with sleep. If anything, he looked even fiercer. For all Fargo knew, Sharp Knife was fighting his enemies in his dreams. The Trailsman considered the best course of action, then moved fast when Sharp Knife stirred and his eyes flickered open.

Before the Apache chief could cry out, Fargo clamped one hand over the man's mouth. With his other he grabbed Sharp Knife's nose and closed the nostrils. The more Sharp Knife struggled, the quicker the air trapped in his lungs was exhausted. The thrashing about died down, but Fargo worried that it was a trick. He held onto nose and mouth for another thirty seconds to be sure Sharp Knife was unconscious.

Carefully releasing his grip, Fargo rocked back on his heels. Sharp Knife did not stir. Grabbing the Apache under the arms, Fargo heaved and slung the man over his shoulder. The hard part of the capture lay ahead as Fargo carefully picked his way back through the camp with the Indians sleeping all around. The slightest sound would awaken them. If that happened, Fargo knew he wouldn't have a chance.

He reached the edge of the camp and then the fat hit the fire. The sleeping sentry awoke, either because he had heard something or a newfound sense of duty brought him back to his post. A wordless cry rang out behind Fargo, forcing him to pick up the pace. With the heavy Apache chief over his shoulder, Fargo could not run as fast as he needed to escape.

Bullets nipped at his legs. One creased his thigh, bringing him to his knees. As he fell, Sharp Knife tumbled from his shoulder onto the ground. The impact brought the war chief to his senses. A dozen possible outcomes flashed through Fargo's mind. None of them ended with him escaping alive unless he abandoned Sharp Knife and made a run for it.

Fargo hated to leave the chief when he had come so close, but the sound of almost a dozen angry Apaches behind him lent speed to his feet. He vaulted over the patch of cactus, then sprinted to get to his horse.

He mounted and rode off, thinking the Apaches would not come after him in the dark. He was wrong.

# 5

They never stopped chasing him. Fargo kept riding into the hottest, driest desert he had ever seen. Every trick he had ever learned he used to throw off the Apaches on his trail. Nothing worked. He realized how angry he had made Sharp Knife by sneaking into his camp and kidnapping him under the noses of his braves. Fargo knew why Sharp Knife kept after him with such fierce determination, but he didn't have to like it.

If the shoe had been on the other foot, Fargo would have stopped at nothing to capture Sharp Knife and bring him to justice.

His water had given out just before sunrise when he took a fifteen-minute rest. The Ovaro wobbled as it walked, forcing Fargo to walk alongside the horse rather than ride. When the sun poked its fiery eye above the horizon, Fargo wondered how much longer he would last. His mouth had turned into a desert on its own. Even rolling the smooth pebble around no longer worked to produce saliva. Every step added a few tons of lead to his feet until he was staggering, half holding onto his horse and half falling.

He had last seen the Apaches around midnight and knew they had to be closing the gap. They knew all the watering holes, even in the middle of this inferno, and he did not. Still strong, the Indians would soon find him. He vowed they would have a fight on their hands when they did. Fargo would not die without taking at least one of the Mescaleros with him—preferably Sharp Knife.

The sand crunched under his boot soles and became

increasingly hot as the sun rose. Fargo hunted for shade, any shade, but it was nowhere to be found. He might collapse and put his head under the dubious shelter of a mesquite or low-growing bush, but what of his horse? There was no shade for the horse, and Fargo would not rest if he couldn't be sure the Ovaro was taken care of.

He kept moving. One step. Another. His knees turned weak, but he kept going, looking for a place to make his stand against the Apaches. The heat mounted until it felt as if liquid fire gusted into his lungs. Fargo kept walking.

Lips cracked and skin feeling as if it were turning to leather, Fargo squinted at the horizon. His heart raced. Four dark shapes moved in front of him. Somehow the Apaches had circled—or had he gotten turned around? The sun hammered at his back, showing which way was east.

"They got in front of me. Don't know how. They did," he said in a barely audible voice that caused the horse to turn and look at him. "Fight 'em. Need to . . . fight."

Fargo clamped his hand over the butt of his six-shooter but did not draw it. The six-gun weighed about three pounds, and he was not sure how long he could hold it up. He wanted to lure the Indians closer before he threw down on them, before he started the last fight of his life.

Hands trembling, legs giving out, Fargo dropped to his knees. The four shapes grew larger and larger and larger as they approached. Fargo squinted and shielded his eyes with his hand. Then he laughed.

"A mirage. Nothing but a mirage." Never in his life had he seen anything so funny. The horses had long, knobby legs and were about the ugliest things he had ever seen. And tall! They stood fifteen or twenty hands high. Not even a Percheron was that big. The horses looked as if they had been put together by a one-armed carpenter from a description given him by a blind man.

Fargo laughed and tried to pull his six-gun. When his target made a curious braying noise completely unlike any mule he had ever heard, Fargo sank down and sat cross-legged. The mirage towered over him, then spat at him. The spittle knocked him flat on his back. The six-shooter slipped from his grip, and he lay staring up at the cloudless blue sky, sure he was going mad. The mirage even smelled bad.

From a long ways off Fargo heard voices.

"Why are you laughing? Never seen a man dying of thirst in the middle of the desert who laughed about it."

"Funny horses," Fargo croaked. Then he choked as water ran over his lips. He rubbed the wondrous water all over his dusty face, relishing the feel of mud forming on his cheeks and forehead. It had been so long since he had sweated even a drop. The water ran in rivers and cooled him. Then he found the canteen and drank, gulping down the contents.

"Whoa, careful. Don't want you bloating like a horse," the man holding the canteen said. He pulled it away from Fargo, who fought weakly to keep it. "Well, all right. Just a few drops more right now. You can have more if you don't puke out your guts."

"Too thirsty to do that," Fargo said, his senses returning. Or were they? The mirage did not leave. If anything, it became even stranger. He looked to his benefactor and saw the man wore corporal's stripes and strange headgear.

"Where'd you get that sombrero?" Fargo asked, staring at the beige round cap with the white canvas flap falling down behind to protect the man's neck from the burning sun.

"From the Levant. Same place we got the camels."

"Camels?"

"You're further gone than I thought." This time the three soldiers with the corporal laughed. "You mistook the camels for horses?" This brought forth a new round of laughter at his expense. Fargo did not care. He was alive and the corporal let him drink more from the canteen.

"I'm running from Sharp Knife and his renegades," Fargo said, finishing the last precious drop of water in the canteen. He tossed it back to the soldier. "They've been after me for three days." Fargo hesitated. Was it only three days? Or longer? He had lost track of time.

Staying alive had become a minute-to-minute pursuit, and the passage of hours and days had become meaningless.

"We're hunting for him," the corporal said. "We're out of Fort Davis. I'm Corporal Williams. Jerome Williams, and these misfits are . . . hell, why do you care who they are?" The corporal laughed and made an obscene gesture to his men.

"I was headed for Fort Davis a couple weeks back," Fargo said, not sure of the exact time anymore. The Cleary family massacre, Goldman dying, the lieutenant being ambushed, Sharp Knife, it all blended in a confusing swirl in his head.

"You haven't been out here without water that long," the corporal said. "No one could survive that long, unless you got turned around and only just ran short of water."

"It's a long story." Fargo looked up at a soldier with a leg curled around the camel's hump, sitting on the peculiar saddle as if it was the most natural thing in the world. "You see any riders?" Fargo called to the soldier.

"Nothing but heat shimmer in all directions. Same as always."

"Keep a sharp eye out," Fargo said. He took a canteen from another soldier and drank more slowly this time. A hard knot formed in the pit of his stomach from too much water, but Fargo couldn't stop himself. His entire body screamed for moisture.

"You're danged lucky. We'll get you back to Fort Davis. Wild Rose Pass isn't far off. Once through it, the fort's not more'n fifteen miles off at the mouth of Limpia Canyon."

Fargo stood and put his hand against the side of the towering camel. The animal turned and snapped at him with its buck teeth. Missing him, it spat.

"They're nasty beasts, mister. Best to let 'em be until they get to know you."

"Where'd they come from?"

"Secretary of War Davis decided back in '54 they would be perfect for desert patrols," the corporal said. The way he spoke told Fargo the verdict wasn't in yet on how useful the snapping, spitting animals were chasing Apaches.

"Jeff Davis has pee-cue-liar ideas," opined the trooper mounted on the camel in front of Fargo. "Don't rightly know why they got money for shippin' these monsters halfway 'round the world but we don't get paid regular. Might be his ex-peer-a-mint didn't sit well, which is why he went back to bein' senator."

Fargo had to smile at this. He remembered Captain Murchison's complaints about supply and salary for his troopers. Out West, all the posts suffered under the same handicaps. The soldiers at Fort Davis had the added burden of riding about the strangest critter Fargo had ever seen in his life.

"If you climb up, you can ride behind me," the corporal said.

"I prefer a horse," Fargo said. Then he saw how weak the Ovaro was. It was suffering as badly from lack of water as he was. Riding was out of the question. Fargo shrugged, then asked, "How do I get up there?"

The corporal smirked and Fargo found out why. The camel bellowed and dropped to its knees when the soldier whacked it smartly with a riding crop.

"Going up," the corporal said, indicating Fargo should position himself over the hard lump in the middle of the camel's back.

By the time they reached Fort Davis, Fargo was as close to being seasick as he ever intended on getting.

"I expected something different," Fargo said, seeing Fort Davis for the first time. No stockade walls protected the fort. Only a low adobe wall circled it, probably to keep the poultry in the compound. The buildings were well maintained, and alert guards watched from the corners of the fort.

"That there's Limpia Canyon," the corporal said, pointing at the mouth of the canyon opening behind the fort surgery and barracks on the west side. "We got an entire squad standing guard there. Too many times the Indians have tried sneaking up on us through that canyon."

"Why not put up a garrison wall?"

"Out of adobe? If you hadn't noticed, there's not much wood in these parts. This works just fine for us."

"As long as the Indians cooperate," Fargo said.

"As long as they don't get more guns," Corporal Williams said.

"That's something I need to speak to your commander about," Fargo said. "The Apaches on my tail have been buying guns from a man named Big Red Frederickson."

"Frederickson." The corporal spat the name. "We know him. Been huntin' him as hard as we have the Apaches. Maybe harder. All he's out for is to make a quick buck. Can't much blame Sharp Knife and his men for not wantin' to be stuck on some reservation. That's like being sent to prison."

"Or to an army post?" asked Fargo, smiling. This got a laugh from the corporal.

"There's the post commander," Williams said, pointing at an officer with shining gold braid in the middle of the parade ground near the flagpole. "Colonel Nolan."

"A good officer?" Fargo took the corporal's hesitation to mean that Nolan was not too well liked. At a remote post as recently built as Fort Davis, officers saw such a command as merely a stepping-stone to better, more important duty.

"Corporal Williams, who is this civilian?" The colonel stood with his balled fists on his hips, glaring up at the camel-mounted corporal.

"Pleased to make your acquaintance, Colonel," Fargo greeted him, taking a dislike to the man right away. Men who spoke past him to another, asking questions he could answer best, always irritated him. "My name's Fargo, and your corporal saved my life. Him and his camel."

As if objecting to the entire world, the camel snorted and shook, almost unseating Fargo. He hung onto the strange saddle, then gave up and slid down the beast's side and landed in front of the colonel. Nolan was shorter than Fargo anticipated, hardly more than five foot six.

"You look the worse for wear," Nolan said, his atti-

tude softening somewhat as he eyed Fargo. "We have
the best water in West Texas. Comes from Limpia
Creek. Go get some."

"Before I do, I need to tell you about Sharp Knife."

This got the colonel's full attention. His eyes narrowed, and he stepped closer to Fargo, as if he might
miss a word.

"I want him, Mr. Fargo. I want him bad. What do you
know of him?"

Fargo related how he had interrupted Frederickson
dealing rifles to the Mescaleros and how Sharp Knife
had chased him halfway across West Texas.

"You knocked him out and carried him out of the
Apaches' camp?" Nolan stared at Fargo as if he thought
he had heard the world's tallest tale.

"I almost made it, but the sentry woke up. I stung
Sharp Knife's honor something fierce, which might be
why he's willing to put aside whatever mischief he was
up to."

"Oh, he's up to what you call mischief," Nolan said,
his lips thinning to a line. "Fort Davis was built five
years ago to protect the Butterfield Overland Stage
route between San Antonio and the Hueco Tanks station outside Franklin, Texas. We've had nothing but
trouble with the Apaches."

"What about road agents?"

"Some, but they steer clear. The few we encounter
run across the Rio Grande and hide in Mexico beyond
our jurisdiction. Let them rot over there for all I care.
Protecting the settlers at La Limpia and the stagecoach
passengers are my primary duties."

"Settlers?"

"La Limpia has about seventy citizens. Just up the
canyon from the fort," Nolan said, jerking his thumb
over his shoulder and indicating the same area that the
corporal had said was being patrolled endlessly by soldiers watching for Indian sneak attacks.

Fargo nodded. This must have been where the Cleary
family was headed when Sharp Knife's renegade attacked their small wagon train.

"You *really* snatched Sharp Knife from the middle of

his camp?" the corporal asked, ignoring his commander's hot gaze.

"I did," Fargo said, "but what matters most is catching Sharp Knife. I tried and failed then. Next time he won't be so lucky."

"You must be about the best—" Corporal Williams started, only to be cut off by his colonel.

"Tend your camels and get ready to go back out right away," the colonel said sharply. He turned to Fargo. His original gruff behavior had returned. "I have serious business to tend to. A wagon has been attacked."

"A wagon?" asked Fargo, coldness forming in his gut. Settlers came and went all the time. Supply wagons from San Antonio and Fort Stockton had to be common. "Where was it coming from?"

"Fort Stockton. Probably another family of danged fool sodbusters thinking this is the Promised Land," Nolan said brusquely.

"You have a name on them?"

"Of course not. A scout reported the attack just as the corporal brought you in. Now get over to the mess and drink your fill and enjoy some food. Our cook will fix you up for now, and I'll figure out what to do with you later."

"The corporal's going back out to see what happened to the wagon?" asked Fargo.

"Yes." The colonel glared at him for taking up his precious time. "I don't suppose you want to go out with him," Nolan said sarcastically.

"I reckon I do, Colonel. Thanks for making the offer."

Fargo took some satisfaction in seeing the colonel's mouth open and then snap shut. He had robbed the man of speech, at least for a few seconds. The last thing the colonel had expected was a man who had been rescued from the desert to turn around and go back.

Fargo went to get some of the sweet water that had been promised and to see to his Ovaro. The settlers attacked on the road to Fort Davis weren't likely to be the Cleary family, but Fargo had a gut-level feeling that forced him to see firsthand. Just to be sure.

# 6

"You got a burr under your saddle, Mr. Fargo?" asked Corporal Williams. "No sense killin' your horse tryin' to keep up with ole Betty." The soldier patted the shaggy neck of his camel. The camel twisted around and snapped at him, but Williams anticipated the move and was well back from the closing buck teeth.

"The scout only saw the wagon in the distance. They might be holding out and need our help," Fargo said.

"You're not sayin' Jacob did anything wrong, are you?" Williams's voice hardened. "He's as brave as they come, but you haven't seen what he has."

"Is he a friend of yours?" Fargo asked, wishing he could push the Ovaro to a little more speed. But he dared not do it. The horse kept up with the long-legged, rolling camels—barely—and Fargo wanted to keep it from dying under him as Marshal Goldman's horse had. The need to reach the wagon worried at him something fierce, though.

"My best friend. Me and Jacob swap stories about the colonel."

"They must be good ones," Fargo said. "The colonel didn't take much of a shine to me. Any reason?"

"You're a distraction. He wants to do such a good job that Jeff Davis settin' there in the Senate takes notice and gets him ordered up to a real command back East. Colonel Nolan can taste a promotion to some general's staff. Rumor has it Davis keeps a close eye on this area since it got named for him."

"Nolan would rather be an adjutant than a field commander?" Fargo wondered how any soldier could prefer toadying up to generals over leading men into a decent fight.

"The colonel's not a man to share much. Don't take it personal, Mr. Fargo. He doesn't like anyone much, himself included."

Fargo stood in the stirrups and shielded his eyes against the fierce glare. Around Fort Stockton the prairie had burned dry this year, making the land look like a desert. Out here in West Texas, it *was* desert. Squinting, he saw tiny dots moving along a distant ridge.

"You see them?" he called to Corporal Williams.

"See what?"

"You've got five feet on me, sitting on that camel. Ahead and to the left of the rocky spire."

"Your eyes are really something, Mr. Fargo," the corporal said, using binoculars to see what Fargo had with his naked eyes. "That's the wagon, and it's not moving. Looks like it threw an axle."

"What about people?" Fargo had seen movement on the ground around the wagon.

"Can't tell how many but they don't look to be too agitated. More like they're trying to get things rolling again."

The wagon and its occupants were visible for most of the next hour. Fargo always marveled at how great the distances were when he could see clearly something that ought to have been within a quick ride. In spite of the camel's apparent heartiness in the desert, Fargo's Ovaro beat them up the final rocky slope to reach the wagon.

Fargo's heart caught in his throat when he saw Abel Cleary holding the long-barreled shotgun like a club. The young man's attitude told him that more than a broken-down wagon had aggravated him.

"Abel," Fargo called. The young man recognized him and relaxed a mite, but not much. He clung to the shotgun for security, as if he needed it against Fargo.

"You come to help again?" Then Abel saw the corporal come over the lip of the hill riding the camel. Abel swung the shotgun around and pointed it at the strange beast. "What 'n the hell's that?"

"Don't cuss, Abel," came a weak voice. "Who's out there?"

"Corporal Williams, Eighth Infantry out of Fort Davis, sir," barked the soldier. He used his crop to urge the camel forward and then to kneel. The corporal slid off the humped animal and walked over to push the shotgun muzzle away. "Don't point that at me, son. Makes me mighty nervous."

Fargo smiled. Corporal Williams was hardly older than Abel Cleary but treated him like a small boy. That was the difference between living on the frontier and growing up in St. Louis.

"Glad to see you, Corporal," said Mr. Cleary. The man struggled to pull himself up into the driver's box from the rear of the wagon. "We need a lot of help."

"What happened?" demanded Fargo. "Where's . . . is everyone all right?" Fargo wanted to ask after Rachel, but doing so without inquiring about the rest of the family would not be proper.

"You must be Skye Fargo. Rachel talked about you. You ran off before I could thank you."

"Rachel?" Fargo saw Joshua helping a woman around the rear of the wagon. The woman looked up, and Fargo saw it was Mrs. Cleary.

"Gone," Mr. Cleary said. "Taken by those damned—"

"You told me not to cuss, Pa," Abel said. "Now you're doing it!"

"Hush your mouth," snapped Mr. Cleary. "We got a busted axle trying to get away from the Indians."

"The Apaches took Rachel?" Fargo looked at Williams. The corporal turned somber.

"Almost three hours ago. I tried to get away, but the mules weren't up to pulling fast enough."

"You can't outrun a war party mounted on horses, sir," the corporal said. Williams waved and got the other three soldiers mounted on their camels up the rocky slope. The stones appeared to bother the camels, making them dance about on their ungainly legs as if they walked on broken glass.

"We fought," Abel said, looking belligerent. "We fought but we ran out of shells."

"The shotgun's empty?" asked Fargo, pointing at the goose gun the young man held. He saw by Abel's expression that using it as a club was the only way it would function as a weapon.

"We held them off as long as we could, but when it got obvious that we'd be goners," Mr. Cleary said, "Rachel tried to decoy them away and they caught her. I wish I was stronger!"

"Why did you and your wife risk the trip again before you were all healed?" asked Fargo.

"We'd spent almost two weeks at Fort Stockton. Don't know how you stand garrison duty, Corporal. No offense, but it was making me mighty edgy. I decided the missus and me were strong enough to reach La Limpia."

"Axle's not broke, Jerome," called a private who had scooted under the wagon. "All that's happened is the hub came off the wheel."

Fargo held down the contempt he felt for pilgrims who knew so little about their wagons that they couldn't tell the difference between a broken axle and a wheel hub coming off. The corporal ordered the private to hunt for the wayward hub while the other two piled rocks and found some way to lever the wagon up to get the wheel back into position.

"Can you describe the Indians who kidnapped Rachel?" Fargo asked.

"Describe them? They were Indians. That's all I know," Mr. Cleary said.

Fargo described Sharp Knife, hoping some other war chief might be out raiding. Rachel had landed in hot water no matter what band of Apache renegades had taken her, but Sharp Knife would be especially vindictive after Fargo had not only humiliated him, but added insult to injury by escaping.

Fargo doubted Sharp Knife would be satisfied with hoping the sun and desert had killed him. The Apache chief would want to see the buzzard-pecked body for himself.

"Got it, Jerome," shouted the private. "I found the hub. It'd rolled down the hill and fetched up 'gainst a cholla."

"You heave the wagon up so I can put that hub on again," the corporal said, gesturing at the three privates to forget about finding a lever and to put their backs to lifting.

"How far back down the trail did the Apaches take Rachel?" Fargo asked Mr. Cleary.

"Not far. See that sand dune? On the other side of it."

"Corporal," Fargo called. "I'm going after the Apaches. Can you see the Clearys to Fort Davis?"

"My pleasure, Mr. Fargo. But I'm not sure you ought to go after the woman on your own, especially if that's really Sharp Knife you're trailing."

"See you back at the fort," Fargo said, urging his horse back along the ragged tracks left by the damaged wagon. He found the spot where the wagon wheel had started coming off, and less than a hundred yards farther the sun-baked ground was chopped up by dozens of horses.

Fargo quickly lost the trail within a mile due to drifting sand and setting sun. The heat vanished with the sun, but it also took away any chance Fargo had of light catching a slightly raised hoofprint and casting a shadow. The dusk brought a growing wind that doomed Fargo's efforts to find the trail at all, but he kept riding. The Apaches had no reason to think anyone would be after them—and Rachel. From what Fargo could tell, the Mescalero renegades were riding directly for the looming Davis Mountains, about ten miles to the north of Fort Davis.

Long after another man would have given up for the night, Fargo kept riding along, following the contours of the land and his own instincts. He saw no trace of the hoofprints, but he *knew*. Fargo also *knew* Sharp Knife was the culprit who had spirited away Rachel Cleary, as surely as if he had seen the Apache war chief with his own eyes.

As determined as he was, Fargo had to rest at midnight. His horse could go no farther. The brief respite from the desert at Fort Davis had not restored the Ovaro to its usual hardiness. Fargo camped, ate a late, cold dinner of jerky along with a can of peaches, then lay back and pulled the blanket up over his shoulders. He fell asleep thinking of Sharp Knife—and Rachel.

Fargo was up before the sun. He shivered in the cold pre-dawn, tended his horse the best he could, and knew they had to find water soon. With luck, by heading in the same direction as the Apaches, he might stumble over one of their hidden watering holes. The easiest way of doing this was to give the Ovaro its head and let it sniff out the precious liquid.

An hour after the sun began heating the parched land, Fargo rode up to a small oasis nestled in the foothills of the Davis Mountains. He tugged hard on the reins to keep his horse from trotting to the shallow pool.

"Whoa, let me check the water," he told the horse. Fargo dropped to one knee and sampled the water. "Not the best I've ever tasted but not alkali or poison," he said. The horse neighed enthusiastically. Fargo let the Ovaro drink for a few minutes, pulled it away while he rinsed the sweat out of his bandanna and shirt, drank some himself before letting the horse drink again. As the horse guzzled away, Fargo scouted the area and found where the Apaches had stopped. A slow smile came to his lips. The tracks were fresh. His instincts were still perfect.

Fargo picked up the pace and followed the new trail into the foothills. When the path turned rockier, he knew the corporal, mounted on a camel, would never be able to come after the Apaches in this terrain. As good as the animals did on soft, shifting sand, the camels' hooves cracked and bled when they crossed rocks.

For the rest of the day Fargo rode, alert to any hint that he came up on the Mescalero renegades. Just before sundown Fargo saw the faint glow of a large campfire ahead along the trail. He found a hollow and left his horse, advancing on foot. Fargo ran his fingers along the cold metal side of the Henry as he spotted an Apache sentry perched high in the rocks above the trail.

It was an easy shot, but Fargo did not take it. Instead, he used his skill to slip by the guard, coming out less than fifty feet from the blazing fire where the Indians had gathered. Fargo lifted the rifle, then lowered it when he saw Sharp Knife. The Apache war chief was poking and prodding Rachel Cleary, as if she were nothing but a prize heifer being sold off.

She recoiled every time Sharp Knife touched her, which amused the Apache. Fargo saw that her hands were bound behind her back and hobbles had been wrapped around her ankles. She could walk slowly, but running was out of the question. The woman would trip and fall if she tried.

Fargo circled the camp to come up behind Rachel and Sharp Knife, intent on the other Indians. They all seemed on edge. Many were leaning against their rifles. Others worked to load six-shooters and then thrust them into their belts. Fargo saw how they were prepared to fight, and that made rescuing Rachel even more difficult.

He flopped on his belly and was wiggling like a snake toward the woman when Sharp Knife suddenly turned and lifted his rifle high in the air.

"Hee-ya!" the Apache chief cried. This galvanized the renegades. Many sprang to their feet. Others faded into the shadows. From where Fargo lay, he realized they were preparing an ambush. He wanted to crawl back into deeper shadows but was caught. Sharp Knife stood less than ten feet away, between him and Rachel. Three braves joined their chief, making the attack Fargo had intended too risky.

"What are you doing?" demanded Rachel. Fargo wanted to caution her, to tell her to hold her tongue. Insulting Sharp Knife guaranteed painful torture. "Tell me what's going on."

Sharp Knife slapped her across the face, knocking her to her knees.

"Silence," the chief said, but he was distracted by the distant clip-clop of approaching horses hooves.

Fargo pushed the Henry in front of him, prepared to use it. Sharp Knife's attention was away from him. That kept him safe for the moment, if he could ever actually be safe surrounded by a dozen Apache warriors prepared for a fight.

"Who is that?" asked Rachel. She cringed when Sharp

Knife moved to hit her again. She subsided and watched as four riders came into the circle of the fire.

Fargo's finger tensed on his rifle's trigger. Frederickson!

Good sense kept him from taking the gunrunner out of the saddle with a quick shot. As much as he wanted Big Red Frederickson brought to justice and the Apache chief returned to the Mescalero reservation up in New Mexico Territory, he had to rescue Rachel first. Getting killed while she was still Sharp Knife's prisoner wouldn't serve either of them.

Sharp Knife shoved Rachel forward. She hobbled over to stand beside Frederickson, who smiled wickedly.

"You know my price, Sharp Knife. I thank you for meeting it."

"What're you saying? What's happening?" the woman demanded.

"Where?" was all Sharp Knife asked Frederickson.

"Send a couple of your boys, them fellows you got sighting down their rifles at me and my gang, back along the trail about a mile. There's an entire wagon filled with Spencers stolen from the Fort Stockton armory."

Fargo seethed at the idea that another sale of rifles was going on and he could not do anything about it. With enough weapons, Sharp Knife could turn the desert red with the blood of soldiers and settlers. From the feral grin on the war chief's face, he intended to do just that. Fargo sighted, but did not know whether to shoot Frederickson or the Apache chief.

In the end, he lay still and tried not to be seen. However many Indians went to check the location of the stolen rifles, enough remained to support Sharp Knife should Frederickson try to double-cross him.

Two sharp reports cut through the still night air, quickly followed by three more.

"We will not deal again," Sharp Knife said to Frederickson.

"Don't matter to me. I've got others interested in buying what I have to sell. But I think you're wrong. You'll come to me because I have what you need. Whenever you want more rifles, you know where to rendezvous."

Frederickson urged his horse forward to Sharp Knife's side. He reached down and tried to get his arm around Rachel's shoulders.

"What are you doing, you animal?"

"I like 'em with a bit of fire," Frederickson said, grinning crookedly. Then the smile faded. "But not too much. Get her up behind me."

Sharp Knife bristled at being ordered around. Then he grabbed Rachel around the waist and heaved her belly-down behind Frederickson. The gunrunner slapped Rachel on the rear.

"You keep quiet. Wouldn't want you falling off in the dark. The rattlers might eat you!"

The threat of snakes caused Sharp Knife to step away. Frederickson laughed harshly, wheeled his horse, and trotted off with Rachel kicking futilely. The hobbles kept her from putting up too much of a fight.

Fargo's finger tensed on the Henry's trigger again. He had only a fraction of a second to shoot Frederickson out of the saddle. But he would have had to shoot the gunrunner in the back. The slight hesitation lost him his chance at a shot.

He swiveled around to get Sharp Knife in his sights, but the Apache chief moved fast, jumping the bonfire and running to his horse on the far side of the camp. All around, Fargo heard the Apaches leaving their hiding places and preparing to ride.

In less than a minute, he was alone in the camp.

# 7

What was he going to do? Fargo slapped the stock of his Henry and angrily stalked around the campsite wondering what his plan should be. He owed Sharp Knife for a list of crimes including murdering Goldman and kidnapping Rachel. The chief didn't know Fargo was within a hundred miles—or even alive—and would fall quickly. Fargo knew it. But Frederickson had taken Rachel in exchange for stolen Army rifles. Fargo owed the gunrunner retribution also.

More.

As much as he would like to put an end to Sharp Knife's depredation, Fargo knew he had to rescue Rachel first. Frederickson was not the kind of man to remain encumbered by a struggling woman for long. He would discard her eventually, after he used her and tired of her. Fargo had to save her from such disgrace before he even thought of bringing in Sharp Knife.

He rummaged about the Apache camp, hoping to find some clue as to where Sharp Knife might go after he picked up the latest shipment of smuggled rifles, but this had been a temporary site. Fargo hurried back to his horse, mounted, and got on Frederickson's trail right away. With Rachel slung over the rump of his horse, the gunrunner wasn't likely to make as good time as he would otherwise.

Fargo guessed Frederickson would take whatever money he had received from the Indians and cross the Rio Grande to spend it. If he tried selling more contraband, Colonel Nolan would eventually run him down.

Wary about the trail he rode, Fargo watched the rocks

and the rugged, rocky land ahead to be sure Frederickson hadn't left a man or two to guard his back trail. Speed usually counted most in such smuggling, but Frederickson might worry that Sharp Knife would double-cross him. Less than twenty minutes of riding brought Fargo to a sandy-bottomed arroyo. It took him more than a half hour of crawling around on hands and knees to understand what had happened there.

The wagon, probably loaded with the stolen rifles, had waited with no fewer than six mounted men guarding it. The wagon headed off to the south. Again Fargo worried about his chance of saving Rachel. The Indians would do more than hurrah a town with those rifles. They would kill anyone in a wagon train or on a stagecoach they found and make life unbearable from Fort Quitman to the north all the way southeast to San Antonio. Colonel Nolan had to be told of the danger the troopers at Fort Davis faced.

After Rachel was safe.

Fargo went in the other direction, following the tracks of the shod horses. In the dark it took more than his expertise to stay on the trail. Every bit of his skill coupled with luck brought him to a rise after an hour of riding. His nose caught the scent of burning mesquite, and he knew Frederickson's men had gone to ground for the night.

He slowly turned, missing nothing, until he found a faint flicker of light through the sparse mountain vegetation.

"Got you," Fargo said, hope surging. He had sneaked into an Apache camp without any of the wily braves noticing him. It would be even easier getting into the gunrunners' camp. The hard part came in getting Rachel free and escaping with her.

She was a greenhorn and not used to riding, even if he managed to steal a horse for her. Worse, Fargo had no idea what condition she was in. Frederickson had seemed mighty anxious to be with such a lovely woman, and he did not look like a man used to gentle ways.

First, however, Fargo had to rescue her. With Frederickson's entire gang in the camp, that would not be easy.

Fargo rode closer, spotted a sentry, avoided him, and then advanced on foot. When he got close enough to see the men gathered around the fire, he knew he had found Frederickson's gang. He recognized several of the gunrunners, and when their leader stood, Fargo was positive.

But where was Rachel?

He feared that Frederickson had already used the woman and then killed her, although Fargo had not seen any evidence of her body as he trailed the gang. In the dark he might have missed it, but he did not think so. Coyotes coming to feed would have shown him the location of the sorry crime.

"Men, we've been real successful these past few weeks."

A cheer went up. Frederickson grinned broadly as he basked in the adulation.

"We made a pile of money, but the time's ripe to move on. Sharp Knife's going to turn the whole country red with spilled blood."

"But we can keep supplyin' him guns and ammo," spoke up a rough-looking customer. "And whiskey. We can sell him gallons."

"You want to be around a bunch of liquored-up Indians?" asked Frederickson. "I don't. I'm saying we should split up or maybe move north into New Mexico. Trouble's brewing there, trouble we can get rich on."

Fargo seethed. The gunrunner cared nothing for the lives lost thanks to his illegal activities. Frederickson had to be stopped—after Rachel Cleary was rescued.

Moving carefully, using the sparse vegetation for cover the best he could, Fargo skirted the camp hunting for wherever Frederickson had left the woman. He heard soft crying. Rachel wasn't far off. He dropped to his belly and snaked his way forward. The wind picked up, whistling up and down the Davis Mountain canyons, covering any slight sounds he might make. Fargo got within a couple of feet of the bound woman without her seeing or hearing him.

"Rachel," he whispered. She jumped as if he had stuck her with a pin.

"Skye!"

"Not so loud. Are you all right?"

"You mean, has he had his way with me?" She looked grim. "Not yet. I could kill him! I never felt this way before, wanting to kill someone. But I'd cut his throat with a dull knife. I'd—"

"Hush," Fargo said, drawing his Arkansas toothpick and slicing through the ropes holding her. He let Rachel rub circulation back into her hands while he worked on the rope hobbles around her ankles. He couldn't help noticing the way her skirt was torn, revealing her shapely ankles and legs. A quick slash with his knife cut through the ropes holding her prisoner.

"What are we going to do, Skye?" Rachel turned to him, then threw her arms around his neck and buried her face in his shoulder. He felt hot, wet tears on his shirt.

"We get away. There's no time for crying. Where are the horses? You have to get a mount." A plan took shape, but Fargo knew luck had to be with him to make it work. "Can you ride a horse?"

"I can because I have to," she answered gamely. This put Fargo on guard. Rachel was willing but lacked the horsemanship skills needed for them to simply ride away.

"Come on," he said, taking her hand and leading her from the camp. When they were twenty yards farther into the mountains, Fargo asked, "When was Frederickson going to . . ."

"Rape me?" She finished for him with a bitterness that told Fargo she would do anything to even the score with the gunrunner. He needed that determination if they were going to escape.

"When?"

"He was basking in the worship of his men for being ever so clever," she said in a steely-edged tone. "Then he was going to rape me and pass me around for all of them to u-u-use." Rachel shuddered and clung to herself, withdrawing from him.

"The horses," Fargo said, focusing her attention on other problems. "Where are they?"

"Near that rock. I think there's a natural corral."

Fargo swore under his breath. He had hoped to steal a horse for Rachel, then drive off the rest to give them a head start. By the time Frederickson's gang had recaptured their horses, Fargo and Rachel could have been miles away. But if the horses were penned in a rock corral, getting the horses out a narrow opening would cause such a ruckus it would be dangerous even to try. He had to think of another trick.

"Listen, I'm going to spook them. They'll chase me, but I will get away from them and come for you. You have to hide until then."

"Don't leave me, Skye. Please!"

"You can't ride good enough," he said harshly. "You'll be all right."

"I wish I had a gun."

Fargo hesitated, then shoved his Henry into her hands. "Here. Just be sure who you're shooting."

"I wouldn't shoot you, Skye. Ever!"

She threw her arms around his neck and impulsively kissed him full on the lips.

"Down there," he said. "Hide until I get back. It might be an hour or longer, but I'll come for you." He wondered how long Rachel would wait if he didn't make it. Not too long, he hoped, because that meant Frederickson would have killed him and would be coming back after his booty.

Fargo saw her to a safe spot, got his bearings so he could find her quickly later, then set out on what might be the ride of his life. He reached the stony corral and saw she had accurately described it. Ropes across a narrow opening efficiently penned a dozen horses in a rock-walled pen. Fargo used his knife to cut the ropes, then went into the pen and grabbed the first horse he came to.

The horse reared and tried to kick him. He evaded the hooves and vaulted bareback onto the horse. Then he calmed the horse enough to grab the bridle of another horse.

"Yee-haw!" he shouted, shooting out the narrow gap and through the gunrunners' camp. The horse's hooves scattered the fire and left Frederickson and his men in total disarray. Fargo rode so fast no one had the chance even to pull out a six-shooter and shoot at him.

Then he was surrounded by the darkness of the Davis Mountains. Head low and maintaining a firm grasp on the other horse's bridle, he galloped into the night. Behind, he heard loud, angry shouts and Frederickson ordering his men to mount up and go after the horse thief. Fargo doubted any of the outlaws even knew who had run off with the horses. All the better if they thought an Apache brave had done the deed.

"Confusion to my enemies," Fargo muttered.

He galloped until his horse began to falter. Slowing to a more sustainable gait, Fargo tugged the second horse up even with him. He gathered himself and then jumped. His strong legs closed around the second horse. When he was secure, he used the reins as a switch on the first horse's rump.

The horse neighed and rocketed once more into the night, this time free of a heavy rider. Fargo reined back and quickly rode at an angle. Let Frederickson and his men chase the other horse. He had a rendezvous with a lovely woman fearing for her life.

Fargo meandered through the rocky terrain as he doubled back. Some distance off he heard riders going after the now riderless horse. He did not think this trick would occupy Frederickson's gang for long, making it necessary to pick up Rachel so the two of them could take off in another direction. Sooner or later Frederickson would get tired of hunting his lost spoils. Even a woman as lovely as Rachel Cleary would cease being a lure if the gunrunner thought time was running out for him. Everything he had said to his men around the campfire told Fargo how much Frederickson wanted to get the hell out of West Texas.

Fargo approached the tumble of rock where he had left Rachel. He worried she might get gun happy and shoot because he was approaching from the opposite direction he had taken when he left her. Jumping down, he walked toward the rocks, careful not to make any sound that might spook her.

He saw the woman huddled over, clutching the rifle and pointing it toward the gunrunners' camp.

"Ready?" he asked, putting his hand on her shoulder. The dark-haired woman yelped and swung the Henry around, trying to poke the muzzle into his belly. Fargo caught the barrel and held it away. His eyes met with her frightened, bright blue ones. "It's all right," he said, as if soothing a spirited horse.

"Skye, I didn't hear you come up. You frightened me!"

"Frederickson and his boys are out chasing a riderless horse, but they'll be back soon. I don't want to be anywhere near here when they get back because they're going to be madder than wet hens."

"He should be hanged," she said fiercely.

"I can't argue that. If I were on a jury, I'd convict him, but we're a mighty long ways from a courtroom. If we ever want to see him tried, we'll have to keep away from him and let the cavalry catch him."

He silently handed her the reins of the horse he had ridden. She took them, swallowed, and then gamely said, "I've never ridden bareback before."

"Now's not a good time to learn, but there's not much choice," he said. Fargo wasn't going back into the camp to steal the tack for her. "I'll get my horse and be back in a few minutes. Watch who you're pointing the rifle at."

He slipped away as silent as a shadow and fetched his Ovaro. Fargo considered letting Rachel ride his horse with its saddle, then decided against it. The Ovaro was rested and used to carrying his heavier weight. The other horse had been ridden hard and might prefer the lighter load with Rachel astride its back.

Fargo wasted no time returning to the woman, poised on a rock, looking apprehensive about climbing onto the horse. She smiled weakly, then reached down and ripped her skirt so she could ride more easily. Torn skirt flapping, she dropped onto the horse and immediately worked the reins to keep it from trying to buck her off.

"You're a natural horsewoman," Fargo said, eyeing

her. He couldn't keep from staring at her bare legs, gleaming like silver in the pale light of the rising sun.

"Let's go, Skye. I don't want them to catch us." She shuddered at the idea of being Frederickson's prisoner again, turned the horse, and started off to the west. Fargo decided this was as good a direction as any, since the gunrunners were likely scattered all over the countryside to the east.

He trotted along after her, enjoying the sight of her skirt flapping away from her shapely legs. As they rode hour after hour, Rachel's skirt tore a little more, revealing increasing amounts of bare flesh all the way up to her thighs. Fargo tried to ignore the lovely sight but couldn't. Rachel was a gorgeous woman, high-spirited and courageous. She rode with her head high and shoulders back, showing off her breasts.

She turned and looked at him, a smile dancing on her lips.

"You see something, Skye?"

"Yes," he said.

"Something dangerous?" Her voice was teasing. She knew he was watching her closely and admiring what he saw. She shrugged her shoulders, causing her breasts to jiggle just a little more. The bouncing movement from being on horseback was enough to torment Fargo, but this added to his dilemma.

"Something real dangerous," he said, riding alongside her. Somehow, the top buttons on her blouse had popped off. It might have been from the strain of riding bareback for the first time, or she might have torn them climbing onto the horse. Whatever the reason, they let her blouse gape wide, revealing the snowy mounds of her breasts.

"Are they after us?" she asked.

"They never picked up the trail," Fargo said. "Frederickson might have decided to just keep riding. He could be in New Mexico by now."

"Then we can stop and rest? I'm getting tired."

"Sorry. I forgot you're not used to riding like this."

"I know why you forgot, too. You were enjoying staring at me."

They halted. Rachel slid her bare leg over the horse and jumped to the ground. She looked up at him.

"Don't deny you were more interested in watching me than in worrying about anyone on our trail."

Fargo tethered the horses, giving them a rest after the long hours of steady retreat from the gunrunners' camp.

"If I said that's not true, I'd be lying," he said.

"And you don't lie, do you, Skye?"

"That's not my way."

She grinned and stepped closer. He thought she wanted him to kiss her, but as he bent over, Rachel spun around quickly and thrust her butt in his direction.

"I'm so sore from riding," she said. "I'm so sore that it would feel good if someone massaged all that aching flesh." Rachel hiked her skirt and revealed a frilly undergarment covering her rump. She slowly pulled it down so Fargo could see her nakedness.

He reached out and grabbed a double handful of her buttocks. He was worried she had meant something else, but Rachel sighed and began moving her hips so he would get the idea. He started massaging Rachel's ass and got a contented purr from the woman.

"That feels so good, Skye. Keep doing it. I love the feel of your hands on me." She widened her stance, and somehow Fargo's hand moved between her legs and found the tangled nest there was already damp with her inner oils. Rachel was excited and wanted him as much as he did her.

He continued to rub and knead the tight flesh of her backside, growing more excited as he did. After a few minutes, Rachel turned and faced him, saying softly, "Is there any part of you that's stiff, Skye? Any part I need to massage?"

Her hands rubbed seductively over his crotch. Fargo felt uncomfortably confined, but this did not last long because the lovely woman had unbuttoned his trousers and grabbed the hard shaft springing forth.

"I thought so," Rachel said, stroking up and down the hardness. "You're stiff."

He kissed her. She returned the kiss with a passion that startled him. When her tongue sneaked forth and dueled with his tongue, he was ready for her. They had been through much together and had survived. They had left death behind, and it was time to celebrate life.

Reaching down, he caught her rump. Moving his hand lower over her bare skin, he lifted her leg so their crotches pressed together intimately. He felt his manhood rubbing into the aroused woman's lust-dampened sex lips. Those delicately scalloped pink portals opened as Fargo dipped in, but again Rachel surprised him.

She pulled her leg from his grip and stepped back.

"Sorry, I thought—"

"Not that way, Skye. This way!" Rachel turned and leaned against a rock, her derriere toward him again. "Don't massage it this time. You know what I want!"

"It's what I want, too," he said, stepping up. Fargo reached around her body and caught the woman's breasts, finding the nipples taut and throbbing with every beat of her excited heart. He tweaked the nipples and cupped the fleshy globes in his palms and then moved closer.

The curves of her rump fit perfectly into the sweep of his belly and upper legs. His iron-hard pillar slid lower, touched her nether lips, tasted paradise, and then drove forward. They both gasped in pleasure as he buried himself balls deep in her most intimate recess. Her clinging damp female flesh surrounded him, clutched him, tried to hold him as he slowly reversed his course.

"Fast, hard, Skye, do it! Burn me up inside!"

He teased her with a few more slow thrusts, and then he knew he wouldn't be able to continue. The pressure built in his loins, driving him to give her exactly what she wanted rather than string it out so they could both enjoy the coupling longer. The woman threw her head back and tossed her dark hair over her shoulder before howling like a wild animal. The sound spurred Fargo on to move even faster. Heat burned at his hidden organ and set fire to the powder keg buried deep in his balls.

Faster and faster he moved like some fleshy piston. He squeezed and stroked and tugged and pinched her breasts. And then she began slamming her buttocks back to meet his every inward thrust.

"Yes, oh, yes, yes!" she moaned out.

Fargo felt her body tremble as if she had a fever. She began rotating her hips, stirring his meaty length around inside her like a spoon in a bowl. Then she shoved backward and took him as her ecstasy reached a climax. Fargo grunted. It felt as if she were crushing him with the powerful contractions of her body.

He pumped harder and then felt the white-hot tide rising within him. He spilled his seed and caused a new quiver of desire in the passionate woman's lush body.

She sank down to her knees and put her cheek against the rough rock where she had been leaning.

"Oh, Skye, that was wonderful. Except for . . ." Rachel's voice trailed off.

"Except?" he demanded. "It was great. What didn't you like about it?" Then he saw the wicked smile on her ruby lips and knew she was goading him on to do it again.

He stopped talking and got back to giving her what she wanted.

And what he wanted, too. Fargo wished he got this kind of a reward every time he rescued someone.

# 8

"Do we have to go back?" Rachel asked, snuggling closer to Fargo. Her long fingers stroked over his chest, down to his belly and then lower in an attempt to convince him to spend another day hidden in the Davis Mountains and whiling away the time pleasurably.

Fargo knew that Frederickson and his gang had given up hunting for them by now. He and Rachel had spent two days near a clear running stream, possibly one that fed Limpia Creek near Fort Davis, and had seen only a few rabbits and a half dozen spiraling, diving Harris hawks out hunting for dinner. This was about as close to heaven as he was likely to find with a pretty woman and no one shooting at him.

"We have to get back," he said reluctantly. "Your family's got to be worried about you."

"I'm in good hands," she assured him.

"So am I," Fargo said, stirring slightly as she tried to find a sturdy handhold. He rolled away and got up. The morning sun still lacked the hot bite it would get in only an hour or so. This was the best time to travel.

"You're right, Skye," she said, sitting up and stretching, arms high above her head. She was naked and the movement caused her breasts to flatten slightly. Fargo had to look away. He was responding to her. If they dawdled here for even another hour, he might never want to get the woman back with her family. Rachel was quite a woman.

"I'm not familiar with the mountains, but I think we might be a couple dozen miles north of La Limpia."

"That's where Papa was headed," she said, climbing

into the tattered remains of her clothing. Every move Rachel made beguiled him anew. The clothes hid little and revealed much as she moved around their small campsite. He had insisted on not making a fire, to be sure Frederickson, or even Sharp Knife, did not spot them. The way they had slept spoon fashion had kept them both warm without the need of a fire.

"What did he intend doing there? You said he was a seed merchant in St. Louis. There's not much call for farming in these parts. No water."

"Oh, there's quite a lot of irrigation," she said. "Papa figured to sell more than seed, however. With his business connections, he wanted to start a store supplying not only La Limpia and Fort Davis but also the Butterfield stations north and south of here."

"Ambitious," Fargo said.

"That's Papa. Abel and Joshua agreed with him, but Mama and I wanted to stay in St. Louis. I'm glad he convinced us to come to Texas now."

"You'd have missed out on being attacked by Indians, having your parents shot up, being kidnapped by a renegade Apache and a gunrunner and—"

"And camping under the stars," she finished for him. "That made the other travails worthwhile. Well, almost."

Fargo had to laugh. He knew what she meant.

"Will they be caught?" Rachel asked unexpectedly. "Frederickson and the others with him?"

"Colonel Nolan seems like a determined gent," Fargo said. "He wants to be promoted and thinks Fort Davis is a stepping-stone to somewhere better." That wasn't exactly true, from all Fargo had seen. The colonel considered this a menial assignment, but if he could bring a semblance of law and order to the territory, he would because of the glory that would fall on him.

"I hope my parents aren't too worried," Rachel said.

"We're getting back as quick as we can, without taking any risks. Even if Frederickson has moved on, Sharp Knife is prowling about looking for trouble."

Fargo saw how her excitement at being with him was fading and guilt was replacing it. He knew they could have gone directly back to Fort Davis when he saw that the gunrunners weren't on their trail, but he'd be the world's worst liar if he said he had not enjoyed the last two days—and nights.

They set off, Fargo guiding them by the position of the sun. By sundown they passed through the knee-high wall around Fort Davis for a tearful reunion with Rachel's family.

Corporal Williams was the first to greet Fargo. He hurried forward, his carbine at port arms.

"Hey, Mr. Fargo, you found her! If you'd been in the Army, you'd've got a medal."

"Returning Miss Cleary to her family is reward enough," Fargo said, glancing over at Rachel. The woman blushed.

Under her breath she said, loud enough for only Fargo to hear, "You can collect more than medals anytime you want."

From the direction of the officers' barracks came a heartfelt shout of relief.

"Papa!" cried Rachel, slipping from horseback and running to her father.

"That's one mighty fine-looking woman," the corporal said, licking his lips. " 'Bout nekkid, too, the way her clothes got ripped." He turned and stared at Fargo. The corporal's eyes went wide, and he started to say something more but nothing came out.

"She's safe, Corporal," Fargo assured the man.

"Uh, yes, sir, reckon she's been in good hands. *Real* good hands," the corporal said, grinning. The smile faded. "The colonel wanted to see you if you ever got back. There's some news he wants to pass along."

Fargo watched as Rachel's mother hurried from the barracks. The three hugged and kissed. Then her two brothers came running up and the family went toward the mess hall. Fargo's belly complained a mite from lack of food, but curiosity was getting the better of him. He wanted to hear what Colonel Nolan had to say. Food could wait, especially since he did not want to intrude on the Cleary family reunion.

He dismounted and went to the commander's office. The door was open to let the cool night air blow through and carry off the day's heat that accumulated inside. Nolan looked up, saw Fargo, and waved him in.

"So you're back, eh? Were you successful, sir?"

Fargo told the colonel about Frederickson, the rifles Sharp Knife had bought from the gunrunner, and Rachel's eventual escape and return.

"Glad to hear the girl's safe," he said brusquely. Nolan sat heavily in the creaking wood chair behind his desk. The officer paused for a moment, then said, "Close the door and I'll tell you my news."

Fargo did as he was told, although the room quickly became stuffy. He settled in a chair and watched the colonel. The officer seemed more animated than before and, if Fargo was any judge, friendlier. Things must have gone the man's way.

"We received good scouting reports about Sharp Knife. Some of it was pure luck, the rest was damned clever work. We can get him, if we use the right bait."

"What might that be, Colonel?" asked Fargo.

"Not what but who." Nolan stared straight at Fargo and smiled. "You, Fargo, you are going to be the lure that lets us capture Sharp Knife."

"I've done a lot of things in my life," Fargo said, "but being used as bait has never been one of them."

"We won't be far away, Mr. Fargo," Corporal Williams assured him. "Me and ole Betty can travel faster than any horse over this sandy terrain. Why, she's got feet the size of dinner plates—larger!—and can run all day without needin' even a shot glass of water."

"Not sure this will come down to a horse race," Fargo said. "If it does, I prefer to rely on my trusty Ovaro." His horse whinnied in gratitude at being favorably compared to a spitting, snarling, rubber-lipped camel. He patted the horse's neck and then settled back to study the lay of the land.

"Over that ridge about five miles off, Fargo," called Colonel Nolan. "That's where the Apaches are camped. You stay here long enough and they'll find you."

"This watering hole is one of theirs?" Fargo looked

around the miniature oasis. "Why aren't they camped here?"

"It is *not* theirs," Nolan said testily. "The water belongs to everyone. They have chosen a somewhat larger watering hole since there are so many men."

"How many?" Fargo asked. He had neglected to find out the details of the plan when he had agreed to help the cavalry arrest Sharp Knife.

"With the contraband rifles as incentive, Sharp Knife has recruited a larger force than before." Nolan cleared his throat and saw Fargo was going to press him if he did not give a straight answer. "Scouting reports show he has about fifty braves in his band now."

"Fifty fighters and all armed with rifles and plenty of ammunition," sighed Fargo. "Even with every man at Fort Davis in the field, you'll be hard pressed to deal with them."

"Not if we trap them," Nolan said. "If we capture Sharp Knife fast, we'll intimidate the fight right out of them and they'll disperse."

"Let's get on with it," Fargo said. He checked his six-shooter and made certain the Henry's magazine was fully loaded. The supply wagon rattled up, driven by a frightened private. Fargo spoke quietly to settle the man's nerves, then rode ahead of the mule-pulled freight wagon as if he were scouting.

Fargo made no effort to hide his presence. Instead, he sang "Green Grow the Lilacs" loudly and off-key as he rode. The hot sun burned down on him and turned his mouth to cotton, but this time he had plenty of water. He had let his horse drink its fill at the watering hole, now a half mile behind, and had a canteen sloshing with reserve. The wagon rattled along twenty yards behind, the driver even edgier than before they had embarked on what would be a short trip.

The road meandered around, and Fargo dutifully kept to it rather than scouting off to either side as he would if he had been gainfully employed. He knew what he would find.

And he knew the instant the Apaches found him. He saw a single flash from a signal mirror and then nothing.

The careless move put him on guard as he rode down into a low-lying section of the road. Fargo saw how perfect this was for an ambush. The wagon had to pull up-hill if it tried to race ahead or if it tried to retreat. Either way slowed the mules and made the wagon and its driver vulnerable.

In the middle of the dusty bowl Fargo slowed his pace and let the wagon close the distance between them. Sudden movement along both sides of the road, coming from around dunes and across hard, sun-baked sections of the desert, alerted Fargo to the extreme danger. He started to shout a warning to the driver but was too late.

Sharp Knife charged from ahead, directly at Fargo. The Trailsman saw instantly that the Apache war chief recognized him. The Apache warriors might be intent on capturing the wagon and its supplies, but their leader wanted to lift Fargo's scalp.

That would go a long way toward winning back respect among his braves. Fargo slid his six-gun from its holster and fired at the Apaches closest to him. His six-shooter finally came up empty, and he had only winged two of the darting, dodging, whooping Apaches.

Then the trap was sprung. The back of the wagon exploded upward, tarpaulins tossed aside, and a dozen armed soldiers opened up on the attacking Mescaleros.

Sharp Knife probably saw he had led his renegades into a trap, but he was too intent on Fargo. Colonel Nolan had used the right bait. The chief wanted to regain his honor and could do it only if he personally killed Skye Fargo. The Apache chief screeched and came at Fargo with a war lance.

Fargo turned his Ovaro using only his knees so he could draw his Henry, not to fire but to use as a defensive weapon. As Sharp Knife's lance drove forward seeking Fargo's heart, the Trailsman swung his rifle around so the barrel knocked into the wood shaft and deflected it. Fargo felt the steel lance head pass close to his chest, and then he dropped his rifle and dived.

Arms tightening around Sharp Knife, he twisted hard and pulled the Apache from horseback. The two went down in a struggling, kicking, fighting pile on the hard ground. Fargo tried to hang onto Sharp Knife but the Indian was too slippery. Before battle he had greased himself down to give himself the edge in any hand-to-hand fight.

Like this one.

Sharp Knife whipped out a blade and held it. His lips thinned to a line as he went into a fighting crouch.

Fargo drew his Arkansas toothpick and faced the chief, ready to fight to the death.

"You stole my honor," Sharp Knife said as he advanced. "Now I will steal your life!" He lunged. Fargo parried the thrust with his own knife but found this was only part of Sharp Knife's attack. The Indian clawed at him like a mountain lion ripping at a calf's belly. Fargo blocked the man's left hand and kicked, knocking the feet out from under Sharp Knife.

Off balance, Fargo staggered back and recovered, only to find the Apache chief was already on his feet again.

A column of sand sprouted at Sharp Knife's feet. Corporal Williams and the rest of the camel corps had arrived. Williams levered another round into his carbine and called out, "Surrender! Give up or I'll shoot you where you stand!"

The corporal's warning did not stop Sharp Knife. He lunged at Fargo, but the Trailsman was ready. He blocked the knife driving in for his belly, grabbed Sharp Knife's wrist, and twisted hard, throwing the Apache to the ground. Fargo followed him down, his knee driving hard to the exposed belly. Air gushed from Sharp Knife's lungs, and by the time he regained his breath, Fargo's knife was pressing against his throat.

"Go on, kill me. Do not dishonor me more," Sharp Knife grated out between clenched teeth.

Fargo knew the Apache preferred to die in battle, and that was what decided him.

"Corporal, get over here and take possession of your prisoner."

Sharp Knife glared at Fargo, hatred hotter than the hot sun above their heads. The Apache chief had been a terrible enemy before. Now Fargo knew Sharp Knife would hate him until one or the other lay dead in a grave—and beyond.

"You were so brave, Mr. Fargo," Rachel Cleary said, staring at him with adoring blue eyes. Fargo saw how that look changed just a mite when he felt a foot sneaking under the table and crawling up his leg. Rachel tried to look innocent, but he knew better from their time together out on the trail. She was a real vixen when she put her mind to it, and he got the feeling she wanted to show him how wild she could get right now.

Fargo felt uncomfortable with Rachel's parents sitting along the broad table in the mess hall, and the way her two brothers were watching him like hawks, he wasn't in a position to do too much. He shifted but the woman's foot followed, edging up his leg and going for his crotch. Fargo did not want to be too obvious as he reached under the table and caught a trim ankle. This produced a broad smile on Rachel's lovely face because she expected more.

A frown quickly followed when he pushed her foot away.

"I will order a commendation for him," Colonel Nolan said from his position at the head of the table. "However, this solves only part of our problem. As you know, we captured Sharp Knife and three of his braves. We killed two and wounded several more."

"Leaving danged near forty of the red devils out there," Mr. Cleary said. "Is La Limpia going to be safe for me and my family, or do we have to fear another Indian attack?"

"Sharp Knife was a powerful leader," Nolan said, looking irritated at the settler's criticism. "We had hoped to kill or capture more of his braves, but without their leader we feel the Apaches will drift away and not be much of a menace."

"What if another leader steps forward?" timorously asked Rachel's mother. "That might be worse since they would have nothing but revenge on their minds."

"That won't make any raiding worse," Fargo assured her. He did not bother telling her the Apaches were off the reservation and prone to kill anyone and steal everything out of a much greater anger. None of them liked being restricted to the reservations, especially the San Carlos in Arizona Territory, because it took them away from their holy lands in the Sacramento Mountains.

"Thank you for your opinion, Mr. Fargo," Nolan said sarcastically. "He, however, is correct on this point. My primary concern is capturing Red Frederickson and his gunrunners."

Fargo leaped to his feet at the sound of a half dozen shots from outside. He motioned for Rachel and her family to remain where they were, but Joshua and Abel both crowded close behind him. Abel clung to the goose gun as if it were a magic wand that would solve all problems. Fargo was not sure the young man had learned how to use it, much less when to use it.

The darkness near Limpia Canyon was ripped open by the foot-long yellow-orange muzzle flashes of a dozen rifles.

"In the rocks, up the side of the canyon. Could the Apaches have gotten past your guards?" he asked Nolan.

"Impossible. My best men are on duty there. I was worried the Apaches might try rescuing Sharp Knife." Nolan stared at Fargo in horror. Both men broke into a run for the stockade where a pitched, silent battle was in progress.

Fargo made sure the fight turned noisy to draw the attention of the soldiers inside the fort away from the snipers along both rims of the canyon. He fired point-blank into an Apache, who let out a yowl of pain and twisted away from the private who had been standing guard outside the stockade. The soldier was clearly dead, his head split open by a hatchet.

"Get your bugler to sound attack or the alarm or whatever will get the soldiers out," Fargo yelled to Nolan.

Another warrior came out of the shadows and tried to slit his throat. Fargo threw up his arm and caught the sharp-edged knife slash on his left forearm. Blood flowing, he twisted around, shoved his six-shooter into the Indian's belly, and fired. The fight went out of the Apache as he died.

"To your posts, to your posts! All arms, all arms!" shouted Nolan. The din inside Fort Davis was almost overwhelming. The silent fight had turned noisy as the troopers rushed, some half dressed, from their barracks. Waving around their carbines, they poured onto the parade grounds.

"Sergeant," Nolan yelled at some noncom Fargo couldn't see. "Guard the animals. Don't let them run off our horses. Corporal Williams, see to your camels. Lieutenant Prospero, defend the north side of the fort."

Fargo spun in a full circle, hunting for other Apaches. He stood alone in the middle of bloody carnage. Four Indians lay dead at his feet, along with four soldiers. Another trooper leaned against the stockade wall, moaning.

"Where are you hurt?" Fargo asked. The young man—hardly more than a boy—looked up with forlorn eyes. Then he moved his hands and showed Fargo how bad the belly wound was. He was holding himself together after a savage knife slash from his left shoulder to his right hip had opened him up.

"Don't say anything. Just wait and I'll get a medic to you," Fargo said.

"Your arm, sir. Your arm's all cut up," the private said. And then he died.

Fargo looked at his left arm and saw how bloody it was. He still felt no pain, but the bleeding had to be stopped or he would turn cold from blood loss and finally pass out. There were still mountains to climb and frontiers to explore, and the Trailsman intended to find them.

He took the advice he had given the dead soldier and sank down. He pressed the remnants of his buckskin shirt against the long wound as hard as he could and waited, six-shooter on the ground beside him should it be needed. Fargo got a little light-headed but kept his keen eyes hunting for any Apaches still in the compound.

"You got quite a scratch there," said a doctor hurrying up with a bag. Two corpsmen joined him.

"What about the others?" Fargo asked, thinking of the dead private whose only thoughts were for him. That was real bravery.

"We got it under control. Now, this is going to hurt like the dickens."

Fargo was not sure what the doctor poured on the wound, but it didn't hurt like the dickens. It was worse. Woozy, he hardly noticed when the doctor started stitching him up.

"You need some rest. Otherwise, you'll be right as rain in a day or two." The blood-drenched doctor stood, stared at the cloudless night sky and snorted. "Right as rain. It never rains here, 'cept when it does it floods everything. Not like back in Ohio." Muttering to himself, the doctor went in search of other wounded.

Fargo got his strength back and stood. He went to the barred door leading into the stockade. Nolan and two of his junior officers were standing in front of it arguing. Colonel Nolan looked at him and his wound and dismissed both with a toss of his head.

"We got to move him, Colonel," insisted a captain. "If we have to defend the fort with all our men, how can we keep the peace along the Butterfield route? How can we hunt for the gunrunners furnishing them their rifles?"

"Captain McCall's right, sir," piped up a lieutenant who looked older than the captain. "We fight a defensive war and lose, because they can pick us off one by one, or we go after them. The only way we can do that is to get rid of Sharp Knife."

"Get rid of him?" asked Fargo. "You mean, shoot him?"

"Of course not, Fargo," snapped Nolan. "They want to transfer the prisoner to San Antonio."

"They have more men there," insisted Captain McCall. "They also have a federal judge who can try him and hang the son of a bitch legal-like."

"They'll only send him packing back to the Mescalero reservation," the lieutenant said. "Either way, he's out of our hair."

"And you get to keep your hair," Fargo finished for him. The lieutenant turned red with anger. "Do you always pass your duty along to others?"

"What are we going to do with him? Hold him until the circuit judge shows up in a week or a month, sir?" asked the captain. "If the Indians get wind of it, they'll kill the judge—and we can't send a patrol to defend him if we have to guard our own walls constantly. And what of the settlers over in La Limpia?"

"You can go after them, track down the renegades, and arrest them like you did Sharp Knife," Fargo said.

"All right, quiet, let me think." Colonel Nolan locked his hands behind his back and paced like a caged animal. In a minute, he let out a gusty sigh. "Captain McCall's right. We escort the prisoner to San Antonio, where the Army has proper facilities to hold him."

"You'll put the patrol escorting Sharp Knife to San Antonio at risk," Fargo said.

"We'll make certain it's strong enough to see a prisoner to safety, even one as brutal as Sharp Knife. All other patrols will be suspended until the detachment escorting Sharp Knife returns. See to it immediately, Captain."

"Yes, sir!" Captain McCall began barking orders to the soldiers who had clustered around to listen to the argument. Fargo felt weak as a kitten and made his way back to the mess hall, where he could sit and maybe get a cup of coffee to perk him up.

"That was quite a gash you got," Joshua Cleary said, almost in awe. "I saw the doctor sewin' you up. You all right, Mr. Fargo?"

"I'm fine. Where's your brother?" Fargo looked around, panic rising until he spotted Abel Cleary with his parents.

"You mean, 'where's my sister'?" Joshua grinned. "I see how you two look at each other. I'm old enough to know what's goin' on."

"And you ought to be old enough to hold your tongue," Fargo said, not unkindly. He went into the mess hall and collapsed on the bench. He wanted to accompany Captain McCall when he took Sharp Knife south to San Antonio, but he knew the doc was right when he said he wasn't going to be up to riding for a day or two.

Rachel hurried in after Joshua told her how badly Fargo was hurt. She was clearly concerned, and Fargo realized that waiting at Fort Davis for a few more days until he recuperated wasn't going to be that onerous.

"You should wait another day or two, Skye," Rachel said, frowning.

"I've got use of my left hand back," he told her, flexing it to show how dextrous it was.

"I know," she said, her eyes lowering. "I remember last night."

"I want to be sure Sharp Knife goes to San Antonio to stand trial for all he's done to you and your family," Fargo said. "I might be the star witness against him for killing Marshal Goldman, not that they'd let him go if I didn't testify. But it can mean a lot if they hear it from the horse's mouth."

"Horse's mouth?" Rachel said, her blue eyes shining. "Not that, not you. But you certainly possess another more interesting portion of a stallion's anatomy, now that—"

She quieted when Colonel Nolan rode over to them. The colonel glared down at Fargo and said, "You don't have to go." The words said one thing and his tone another. He wanted to be free of all civilians on his post as quickly as possible, and the colonel saw Fargo as nothing but a distraction to his men.

"I might be needed at the trial, Colonel," Fargo said.

"There are camel patrols out between here and a spot twenty miles to the south. Beyond that, the wagon with Sharp Knife is on its own. Captain McCall took along twenty men."

"Are they riding horses or mules?" asked Fargo. He had not seen the patrol leave, having fallen into a deep sleep due to blood loss.

"Mules," the colonel said with some disgust. "There weren't enough horses to go around. The Apaches snuck off with at least thirty head during the attack."

Fargo tried not to show his surprise. He had not heard anything about the horse theft during the Mescaleros' rescue attempt. He nodded in the colonel's direction, mounted, and then touched the brim of his hat as he rode past Rachel Cleary.

"You'll be back, won't you, Skye?" she called.

"Of course," he told her, garnering a sour look from Nolan. He wondered if the officer was sweet on Rachel. That explained the colonel's dislike for him. Fargo rode quickly to put distance between himself and Fort Davis. Captain McCall had been on the trail for three days already. Fargo intended to overtake him and his prisoner in another two.

As Fargo rode, he saw evidence of the camel patrols, but it wasn't until the second day of hard riding that he spotted three soldiers on camels ahead along the road to San Antonio.

"Hey, Mr. Fargo, howdy!" cried Corporal Williams. "I wondered when you'd be along."

"Did McCall say I'd be following him?"

"The captain?" Williams laughed. "Nope, it was the prisoner. Sharp Knife said you wanted to see him die like a dog. I got to thinkin' on it and figured it was true."

"How far ahead are they?"

"I left them at a watering hole yesterday noon. Old Betty drank her fill and is good for another week or two out in the sun. I reckon from the way McCall's men were droopin', they might be slowin' down. You can overtake them by sundown."

"So soon," mused Fargo. That suited him fine. The quicker he got Sharp Knife into the Army prison at San

Antonio and convicted, the sooner he could be back on the trail for Fort Davis. For Fort Davis and Rachel Cleary. He already missed her, and that was unusual. All he usually missed was the wide-open spaces, the tall mountains, and the brisk winds blowing along high-walled canyons.

"You want us to ride with you?"

"No need, Corporal," he told Williams. "You're supposed to be on patrol, not reinforcing McCall's force." Fargo hesitated, seeing the corporal wanted to say something more but was holding back.

"What is it?" Fargo finally asked.

"Can't rightly say. Nothin' I can put my finger on, but it'd be smart of you to keep a sharp eye out."

"Apaches?"

The corporal shrugged and shook his head. "I haven't seen hide nor hair of one, other than Sharp Knife. And he's shackled up tight as can be in the back of the captain's prison wagon. I might be imagining things but there's something in the air—" Williams swatted and dropped a crushed insect to the ground. "Something other than bugs and too danged much heat."

"Thanks, Corporal," Fargo said, infected by the man's uneasiness. He put his heels to the Ovaro's flanks and trotted off.

Before he had gone five miles, he saw the fresh tracks left by the Army wagon. Fargo varied the gait but did not rest, intent on overtaking the cavalry column.

A smile crept onto his lips as he wondered if it was proper calling a soldier astraddle a mule a cavalry trooper. The smile faded when he heard loud cries, quickly followed by a dozen rapid gunshots.

"Giddyup," Fargo cried, putting his heels into the Ovaro's flanks. This time he ran the horse until the flanks were lathered and the valiant horse began to tire. With every thud of the horse's hooves Fargo heard new gunfire, and the reports were mixed in pitch and timbre, telling him the troopers were being attacked by men using different types of rifles.

Smuggled rifles, guns sold them by Big Red Frederickson.

The road wound around and came out between two towering dunes. This was the site of the ambush. Captain McCall had ridden between the sand dunes and found himself attacked from both sides. Rather than push ahead, the officer had chosen to retreat.

That had been a fatal mistake.

McCall and his scouts had missed how the Apaches were massed on this side of the dunes. The first fusillade had been meant to throw the soldiers into disarray. Any of them retreating would be cut to ribbons by the main body of the Mescalero renegades. The best Fargo could tell, McCall had ordered a retreat, guaranteeing his entire force was killed.

Fargo reined back and let his straining horse stop while he studied the battle site. If McCall had tried to outrun the Indians, he might have made it. Fargo doubted it, not with most of the Apaches on rested horses and able to chase the wagon and mule-mounted soldiers, but that was the only hope the captain had had.

Counting, Fargo got up to eighteen dead soldiers. He saw no sign that they had killed even one attacking Apache. The assault had been swift and well planned to rescue Sharp Knife.

"He's going to have competition if he wants to stay war chief," Fargo mused. That did not bode well for the Indian campaign in West Texas. Every young buck would have to show he was more treacherous and blood-thirsty than Sharp Knife. Fargo walked his horse toward the still bodies and looked carefully to be sure no one had survived. Most of the soldiers had been scalped.

Captain McCall had been scalped and mutilated.

The wagon where Sharp Knife had been shackled was overturned and the bolts holding the shackles ripped from the wooden bed.

Fargo looked around, trying to get his bearings. He had not seen the Apaches. He saw no reason for them to continue along the road to San Antonio. If they cut due east, they would be going deeper into Texas and nearer the state capital. Sharp Knife might like the idea of taunting his enemies, but right now the chief would want to lick his wounds and work himself up into a killing rage against everyone around Fort Davis.

The best place to find sanctuary and to recruit more braves off the reservations was across the Rio Grande in Mexico.

Although Fargo thought he knew better, he still turned his tired horse due west toward the river and began his search for the Apaches' trail.

# 10

Fargo considered retracing his path and getting Corporal Williams's patrol after Sharp Knife, then decided there wasn't enough time. The Apaches who had rescued Sharp Knife would not want to stay in the U.S. an instant longer than necessary. They had massacred Captain McCall and his entire company, and they had to know the Army was going to be sharpening their long knives and hungering for red scalps. Better to sneak across the Rio Grande, wait a week or a month, and then return to raid.

Unless Sharp Knife whipped them into a murdering frenzy. Then all hell would be out for lunch throughout West Texas.

The cruel heat wore Fargo down, but he was getting used to it. Now and then he stopped to let his Ovaro rest while he studied the trail. The fleeing Apaches had made no effort to conceal their tracks, telling him he was right about the renegades' intentions. By sundown Fargo was as tired as his horse and curled up by a small cooking fire. An incautious rabbit furnished dinner, and then he slept until a couple hours before sunrise, when he was again on the trail.

Just at dawn Fargo slowed his pace and studied the tracks, wondering what trick Sharp Knife was pulling. A single rider had cut to the north, as if trying to double back on the trail. It looked that way, but Fargo doubted it because of how easily spotted the deviating tracks were.

"Is that you, Sharp Knife, heading to cause more mischief?" Fargo wondered aloud. The main body of riders continued west, heading for refuge in Mexico. Should he chase after most of the riders and let the solitary Apache escape?

He turned and went after the lone rider, not sure if he was following Sharp Knife or another of his band. Either way, Fargo intended to get some valuable information. If he captured one of Sharp Knife's warriors, he might find where in Mexico the Apaches were hiding out. Colonel Nolan might not be authorized to follow across the Rio Grande, but the Trailsman carried all the authorization he needed in his holster.

If he found Sharp Knife at the end of the trail, Fargo knew the game would come to an end. If necessary, either Sharp Knife would die or he would—and Fargo had too many trails left to revisit to let it be him.

It took Fargo less than an hour to overtake the Apache. He grunted in disgust when he saw the Indian was not the Apache war chief but another brave. He had wanted to bring Sharp Knife to justice. Capturing this man only put off the eventual showdown between him and the Apache chief. Fargo pulled his hat lower to shield his eyes and got to the chore of overtaking the warrior.

Cutting to the northwest to put himself between his quarry and the distant Rio Grande, Fargo turned back to the east and found a small watering hole.

"This is where you're coming," Fargo said to himself. He let his horse drink a mite, then led the reluctant Ovaro back out of sight so he could set his trap. The ambush wasn't fancy. It didn't have to be. The Apache rode straight in without scouting the area. He obviously thought he was alone and only the Apaches knew of this small oasis.

As the Apache flopped belly down to drink, Fargo stepped up behind. The Indian saw Fargo's reflection in the water but tried to hide the knowledge.

"No need to pretend you haven't seen me," Fargo said. "I've got a six-shooter aimed at the middle of your back."

The Apache growled something in his own language. Fargo answered in kind.

"Go on, white eyes. Kill me!" the brave said angrily. "I have failed as a warrior."

"Won't argue the point with you," Fargo said. "Catching you was real easy. Just like it will be when I find Sharp Knife down in Villa Acuña."

"We go to Ojinaga!" the brave blurted. He understood then that Fargo had baited him, fishing for details of Sharp Knife's escape. Realizing how he had betrayed his chief, the brave kicked back and tried to knock Fargo to the ground.

One moccasined foot struck Fargo's leg. He turned slightly to keep from going down. He was still on his feet but faced an angry, frightened opponent. The Apache drew his knife and slashed awkwardly. Fargo stepped back, cocked his six-gun, and hoped the Apache would be sensible enough to back down.

The Apache got to his knees in the shallow water. Slipping on the muddy bottom, he desperately threw his knife at Fargo at the same instant the Trailsman fired. The knife bounced harmlessly off Fargo's chest. The bullet caught the Apache brave in the head, knocking him back into the water.

"Damn," Fargo said, going after the Indian. The brave had died instantly when the bullet caught him smack between the eyes. Fargo tugged the dead warrior out of the water to keep from contaminating it. He dumped the brave onto the shore and stared at him, wondering why he had split from the main group.

Fargo searched the brave and found nothing. He had not really expected to find a written note. The Apaches communicated verbally. If this warrior had been sent to negotiate more rifle sales from Frederickson, that message of where and when was lost. Fargo grabbed the Indian's pony and tugged it after him.

"One down, Sharp Knife to go," he told his Ovaro as he mounted. The horse was skittish around the Apache pony but settled down after a mile or two. When he had returned to where the paths had parted, Fargo switched to the pony for an hour, letting his Ovaro rest. Swapping horses periodically allowed him to make better time and overtake Sharp Knife's band three hours after sundown.

He knew he was getting close to the Apaches when the captured pony began rearing and noisily protesting. Fargo guessed the horse scented its equine comrades. Grabbing his rifle, Fargo advanced slowly to be certain he was not tracking some other band of Indians. The horses were unshod, but that did not mean they belonged to Sharp Knife's Mescaleros.

But they did.

He moved close enough to identify the three braves with Sharp Knife. Fargo wondered where the rest had gone. Then he saw the horses in a rude rope corral, standing on limping and favored legs. The Apaches had run their horses almost into the ground attempting to get across the Rio Grande to safety in Ojinaga.

Fargo sat and watched for an hour, wanting to be certain the rest of the renegades weren't out hunting. The way Sharp Knife and the other three sat told him they figured they were alone and not expecting anyone else.

He considered his options. One against four armed Mescalero warriors. Even if Fargo had the drop on them, his chances of capturing them did not bode well. If the tables had been turned, Fargo did not doubt Sharp Knife would have simply opened fire and killed as many as he could. That wasn't the way Fargo lived. Shooting a man in the back was murder, no matter what.

He levered a round into the Henry. Fargo was never quite sure what gave him away. It might have been the distinctive sound a round makes as it enters a firing chamber, but Fargo did not think so. One Apache must have looked up and, eyes sharp and adapted to the dark, spotted him somehow.

The Apaches grabbed for their rifles and turned toward Fargo. He got off a shot that brought down one warrior as Sharp Knife and the other two cut loose a barrage of lead that drove Fargo to cover. He hit the ground, rolled, and kept rolling until he came up behind a creosote bush. Sneaking a quick look around the greasy gray-green bush, Fargo saw a brave sneaking toward him.

When he poked around the bush a second time, he

had his Henry in front of him. Fargo fired, then jumped when the report sounded twice as loud as it should have. He worried the rifle barrel had split or the round had somehow blown apart the firing chamber. Checking the weapon eased his mind. The Henry was a tough, reliable rifle and was in workable condition.

Fargo chanced a look again and saw what had happened. He had hit the approaching brave at the same time the Apache's comrade had fired—into his friend's back. The two slugs had brought down the Indian.

The second Apache looked up from where he had shot his friend in the back. His eyes went wide with anger. He tossed aside his rifle and whipped out his knife, holding it high over his head. With a bull-throated roar, he launched himself in Fargo's direction, intending to vanquish his enemy as personally as he could.

Fargo knew the berserk rage that gripped the Apache would not fade until sated by blood—and maybe not even then. The Apaches mutilated the bodies of those they particularly hated. Fargo knew he would end up as dismembered buzzard bait if he tried to fight the Apache hand to hand. More than this, Fargo knew Sharp Knife was still near.

Even if Sharp Knife had taken to running, Fargo realized he had no time to waste bringing down the charging Indian.

He ducked around the creosote bush, then plunged directly through the center of it. The Apache was distracted by the shaking limbs and lashed at one touching his arm. His attack misdirected, the Apache fell quickly to Fargo when he lifted the butt of his rifle and brought it down hard on the exposed head.

The dull crunch told Fargo the Apache was not going to get up any time soon. Panting harshly, Fargo swung around and went looking for Sharp Knife.

It did not surprise him to find that the war chief had fled.

Fargo ran to his horse and mounted, not bothering with the captured Indian pony now. Speed counted more than endurance. He rode after Sharp Knife, finding the chief's trail heading directly for the Rio Grande and the supposed sanctuary of Mexico on the other side.

This had come down to one-on-one, *mano a mano*, as the Mexicans said. Sharp Knife had a passel of crimes to answer for, and Skye Fargo was the man to bring him in for trial. In the distance echoed the sound of horses hooves. From the curious resonant ring Fargo knew Sharp Knife was close to the river with its tall rocky walls on either side. The Apache chief had to keep riding a mile or more to find a spot to cross here, or so Fargo remembered from Army maps of the area.

He rode onto a rocky river shore and saw he was right. The canyon walls here prevented crossing until the Rio Grande widened. The river boiled and churned, deadly to anyone attempting to traverse it. Sharp Knife had ridden north in an attempt to find a ford.

Fargo took off after him. The darkness hindered him as much as it did Sharp Knife. Fargo had no need to track the chief. There was nowhere else Sharp Knife could run.

The sound of Sharp Knife's horse faded as the rush of the river drowned out such small noises. This put Fargo on guard. He doubted Sharp Knife would abandon his horse for the dubious distraction that would offer. But no noises of riding meant Sharp Knife could be lying in ambush.

Fargo rounded a bend in the river and caught sight of Sharp Knife a half mile ahead, his horse picking its way carefully amid the fist-sized rocks along the river. Pulling out his rifle, Fargo sighted and fired in a smooth motion. The recoil caused his Ovaro to start, but Fargo saw his shot had accomplished its task.

Shooting the Apache from horseback had never been Fargo's intention; even a scum as low as Sharp Knife deserved more than a shot in the back. But the report did cause Sharp Knife's horse to bolt. It stepped between two large rocks, twisted and nearly broke its leg. The horse sank to its knees, tried to stand and then keeled over, throwing the Apache chief in the process. Hurting his foe's horse wasn't the way Fargo wanted to bring in his quarry, but there had been no other way.

Left alone, Sharp Knife would have crossed the river and possibly lost himself in the tangle of vegetation there. Fargo might have found him, but it would have been dangerous, very dangerous considering how wily Sharp Knife had shown himself to be.

Urging his horse forward, Fargo closed on the Mescalero war chief. Sharp Knife looked around, then darted for some rocks a dozen yards away from his fallen horse. Fargo thought Sharp Knife took a rifle with him. Safely hidden behind large boulders damp from the Rio Grande spray, Fargo watched and waited. When it became obvious he could not outwait Sharp Knife, Fargo made sure his horse was securely tethered, then went after the Apache.

The darkness was a boon. He moved unseen from shadow to shadow until he was within a few yards of the rocks where he thought Sharp Knife had sought refuge. Listening hard, Fargo tried to catch any sound Sharp Knife might make and locate the chief that way. The gushing, surging Rio Grande prevented this.

He took a deep breath, steeled himself and then spun around the boulder where Sharp Knife had hidden. Fargo found himself, pointing his rifle at thin air.

Fargo's instinct kicked in, and without hesitation he spun around, lifted his rifle, and fired at a the dim shape atop the next rock. Fargo's round missed Sharp Knife, but he had gotten if off quickly enough to throw off the Apache's as well.

Not waiting to see what Sharp Knife would do next, Fargo launched his attack straight up and over the boulder where the Apache had been. He scrambled fast, his boots finding scant traction. Flopping over the top of the rock, he pointed his Henry down the far side.

Nothing. Again Sharp Knife had eluded him.

Fargo risked standing and looking around. To the west rolled the Rio Grande, spewing up white foam and powerfully surging across rocks and a half-submerged sandbar in the center of the maelstrom. To his left lay the trail back to Sharp Knife's camp, where three of his band lay dead or dying. And to the right rose the steep canyon wall. Dark crevices afforded places to hide, but

Fargo doubted Sharp Knife would do that. The chief had more in common with Fargo than the Trailsman would ever admit.

Determination—and more than a little touch of revenge—drove him.

At that thought, Fargo went into a crouch, spun around, and levered in another round as he tried to see what lay behind him.

A thousand impressions came to him in a rush. Sharp Knife's triumphant face. The rifle bore looking as large as a man's fist. The sharp crack of a rifle firing—and it was not his.

The sudden pain lifted Fargo up and threw him to the side. He hit the stony bank, then pushed to his feet only to crash forward into the river, caught in its strong grip. He was swept downstream by a force too powerful to fight.

The last thing Fargo heard before he hit his head against a submerged rock was Sharp Knife's mocking laughter.

# 11

Over and over Fargo rolled, caught by the powerful current of the Rio Grande. He smashed hard into a rock, stunning him. Then he sputtered and began to fight against the cold, murky water. His hand crashed into a rock and sent a thrill of pain straight to his brain. Memories crashed into his consciousness, and he remembered how he had gotten the wound on his arm, where he was, and all Sharp Knife had done.

Spitting water, he forced his way to the surface. He was driven cruelly into another rock, bent around it, and slipped farther into the center of the fast-running river. Fargo stopped fighting and began to go with the rapid current. When he reached the surface and began breathing regularly, he angled to the shoreline. He needed land under him so he could rest. The battering he received was wearing down his stamina and robbing his arms of strength.

Deliberately moving at a slight angle, he found himself thrown onto the bank when the Rio Grande took a sharp hairpin turn. He tumbled a few feet, then sank to the ground, exhausted. Fargo knew Sharp Knife might be watching. The Apache chief was a deadly shot with his rifle, but Fargo could not force himself to stir for long minutes. When he did, he saw that he had been carried across the river and lay on the Mexican side.

He sucked in long, deep draughts of air. When his strength returned, he walked to the edge of the river. His sharp eyes scanned the far shore for any sign of Sharp Knife. The Apache chief had vanished.

Fargo didn't know whether to count himself lucky on

that score. He wanted the Apache brought to justice, but continuing their duel now might be beyond his endurance. He needed to rest, and eat and sleep—and then sleep some more.

He squatted at the river, letting the current race past. Only when he felt up to it did he again plunge into the charging rapids. Strong strokes took him to the center of the Rio Grande, and again he had to angle to reach the shore. As good a swimmer as he was, the river's current was stronger and utterly tireless.

Flopping ashore on the U.S. side like a beached fish, Fargo lay flat and panted like a dog. He had thought he could reach this side with little effort since he was conscious and not being shot at. How wrong he was! The swim had drained him of all energy.

He crawled a few yards and found a crevice in the steep rock wall. Wedging himself in, Fargo thought to rest a few minutes out of sight. He might have passed out or simply gone to sleep, but eventually he came to when the sun crept close to his feet hours later.

"Sharp Knife," he muttered. His hand touched the shallow groove on the side of his head where the Indian had shot him. The bullet had dazed him so much he had blundered into the Rio Grande and been swept away. He realized this might have saved his life. If Sharp Knife had known his shot had not been a killing one, he would have come after Fargo to finish the chore.

Fargo pulled off the leather thong across the hammer of his six-shooter and drew the gun. It was drenched from his unplanned, extended swim. Drying it and replacing the rounds in the chamber took a while, but Fargo wanted to be sure the Colt was ready for action should he come across Sharp Knife.

His caution was for naught. Fargo found where Sharp Knife had crossed the Rio Grande. The renegade Mescalero was hours ahead of him. Maybe he was heading for Ojinaga or some other rendezvous with his surviving band. Fargo was in no shape to go after him. More than that, he felt a duty to report McCall's death to Colonel Nolan. The Fort Davis commander might already know, but not unless a stagecoach or other traveler had come north along the road. Fargo had noted how little traffic there was these days, owing to the Apache raids.

"You get enough to drink?" he asked his horse. The Ovaro neighed, happy to see him, and jerked hard against the reins tethering it to the rocks. He let the horse loose so it could find grass along the riverbank. While the horse ate, Fargo dipped into his increasingly sparse supplies and did so as well.

"Another reason to go back to Fort Davis," he said, trying to justify his lack of resolve in going after Sharp Knife. Whenever he had ventured into Mexico before, it had not been pleasant. Fargo wanted to be in top shape when he went after Sharp Knife again.

Not rushing, he made his way back along the Rio Grande and eastward when the cliffs allowed. He climbed from the river to high desert and turned toward distant Fort Davis. As the sun began cooking his brains, Fargo sought shelter from the hottest part of the day. He started for a stand of cottonwood trees a mile away, promising not only shade but water as well.

He quickly reined back and studied the ground. On a narrow path leading to what he took to be a watering hole he saw bleached bones poking up out of the sand. More than the evidence of enduring death, Fargo saw a double line dragged through the sand, as if someone had ridden along pulling someone behind.

"No hoofprints," he said, dismounting and studying the sign more carefully. The marks in the ground came from a man, belly down, painfully dragging himself along. The deep ruts so recently furrowed into the sand were caused by the toes of the man's boots. Here and there Fargo saw depressions where fingers might have clawed the ground for traction.

Fargo slid his six-shooter from its holster and advanced warily. Evidence showed someone ahead. From the tracks on the ground the man wouldn't be in any condition to put up a fight, but Fargo had learned a hard lesson well over the years. The man who looked the least likely to put up a fight was probably the most dangerous.

He topped a rise and looked down into a bowl-shaped depression. Stunted trees grew around the shallow pool of cloudy water. Not five feet from the edge lay a man, facedown and unmoving. Fargo looked for a trap and saw only the desperate gent trying to reach the life-giving water—trying and failing by only a few feet.

Fargo came up on the man from the side. Just when Fargo was sure the man had died with his goal in sight, the "corpse" stirred and kicked feebly.

*"Agua,"* came a weak demand.

Fargo went to the man, still cautious. He rolled him over and knew this was no trap. The man's lips were cracked and bleeding. His tongue had begun to swell from lack of water. From his complexion and dress, he was Mexican. His eyelids flickered, and his dark eyes fixed on Fargo.

*"Agua,"* he said. *"Ayudame."* Weakly reaching, he tried to get to the pool of water.

"No," Fargo said. For a brief instant anger and hatred flared in the Mexican's eyes. "It's not that. I don't know you or have a grudge against you," Fargo said hastily. "That's bad water. Alkali. *Agua dañosa.* You drink it and you'll be dead in a few minutes, like all the animals around here."

"Bones. Saw bones, but . . ." The man's voice trailed off.

Fargo lowered the young man's head gently to the damp ground and whistled. His Ovaro came trotting up. The canteen bouncing at the saddle was quickly un-corked and its precious contents dribbled on the dying man's lips.

"Not so much," Fargo said. "You understand English?"

*"Sí,* yes, I do," the man said in a heavy Spanish accent. "I told you I saw the bones."

"Sorry," Fargo said. "I'm not thinking too straight myself." He helped himself to some of the water, then handed the canteen to the man, who accepted it greedily. Then he caught himself and only sipped the water. Fargo knew he could trust him not to drink so fast he'd puke it back up.

"My horse threw me. I do not know how far away."

"I didn't see any horse," Fargo said, looking the man

over. His once fine clothing had been ripped and dirtied by his painful clawing through the desert. From the way his right leg stuck out at a strange angle, Fargo guessed it was broken. When it touched it, the vaquero cried out in pain.

"I need to set that. We're in luck. There are a few trees so I can make a splint after I set it."

"Do what you must. The leg hurts, especially now that I am no longer so thirsty. Thank you." He handed the canteen back, some water remaining. Fargo appreciated such courtesy since they would both need the few drops before they got back to Fort Davis.

"First, I need to look over the leg." Using his Arkansas toothpick, Fargo cut away the man's pants leg. As he had thought, the leg was broken and a piece of ugly white bone protruded through the flesh. Fargo went to work and within a half hour had the leg set, the wound bound and a rude splint put on.

The Mexican had passed out soon after Fargo began working on him. But the man's breathing, ragged at first, evened out, and soon he seemed sleeping rather than unconscious. Fargo left him in the shade of a runty cottonwood while he lounged back and dozed himself.

The sun was setting when Fargo awoke. He stretched and checked his patient. The Mexican's eyes blinked open and fixed on his rescuer with clarity.

"I owe you my life," he said. "My name is Paco."

"Well, Paco, it was my pleasure helping you. Strange how luck that seems bad turns out to be good."

"I did not drink the bad water," Paco said, nodding.

"And I had enough water to save you. Since it's mostly gone now and I don't know where all the watering holes with sweet water in them are, we'll have to make good time getting back to Fort Davis."

"Fort Davis?"

"That's where I'm headed."

"You are a scout for the U.S. Army?"

"Been called worse," Fargo allowed. "No, I just have some important news for the post commander. A detachment from the fort was ambushed, and the officer and all his men were killed."

"I did not do it!"

"I know you didn't," Fargo said, looking sharply at Paco and wondering why he was so quick to deny wrong-doing. "Sharp Knife's band of renegade Apaches were responsible. They rescued their chief and hightailed it across the river into Mexico." Fargo thought a moment, then said, "I'll see you to Fort Davis and then maybe you can show me around Mexico so I can find Sharp Knife."

"No."

Fargo was taken aback by the emphatic refusal.

"What are you saying no to, going to Fort Davis or helping me find Sharp Knife across the river?"

"I will not go to the Army post."

"You don't have much choice, not with that leg of yours and me having the only horse. I have to report to Colonel Nolan. Leaving you alone out here in the desert is a sure way of dying slow-like."

"I will live. I am tough!"

"Tough and with a busted leg. You can't even walk. With no water you'd die in a day or two, shade or not."

"No. I will not go to Fort Davis."

Fargo said nothing, knowing the man would eventually fill in the silence with more of an explanation. He had nothing against helping Paco back across the Rio Grande, but only after he had given Nolan what information he could about Captain McCall's death. The officer had relatives somewhere who should know he had died in the line of duty. If possible, Colonel Nolan would send out a patrol to retrieve McCall's and the rest of his men's bodies for proper military burial. That was necessary for the morale of the entire fort.

"You do not ask why I will not go to Fort Davis?" asked Paco. Fargo kept his silence, watching and wondering about his patient. Paco was younger than he had thought at first. The ravages of the desert had aged him considerably. Cleaning off some of the dirt and getting some shut-eye had perked him up a mite. If Fargo was any judge, Paco was barely in his twenties and from a prosperous background. He spoke English well, wore ex-

**95**

pensive clothing, and his attitude was one of command, not subservience.

"Very well. You helped me once. You must do so again. I am Paco Gonzalo y Rodriguez, and I fled into this terrible desert to escape the *Federales*."

"The Mexican soldiers?"

"Yes. They chase me because . . ." Paco eyed Fargo, as if sizing him up to see if a lie would do. He heaved a sigh and came to the conclusion truth was better with the Trailsman. "They chased me because I am a *bandido* and wanted in every state in northern Mexico."

"You're a road agent?"

"That is another name, yes." Paco stared at Fargo with his fathomless dark eyes. "You will turn me over to the U.S. Army?"

"No, not unless you've committed crimes in this country." Fargo could not tell from Paco's reaction what the answer to that might be if he asked him point-blank. "But I'm heading to Fort Davis and you're coming along with me, no matter what. I can't let you die out here."

"No!"

"You've got no choice, Paco."

"They will recognize me. I am famous! This colonel will turn me over to the Federales, who will torture me and kill me!"

"Colonel Nolan's got a powerful lot on his mind. Taking the time to send you back across the Rio Grande with an armed guard doesn't seem too likely to me."

Fargo heaved the young man up and threw him over his shoulder. Paco fought but was too weak to put up much of a fight. All the starch went out of Paco, and he let Fargo dump him belly down over the saddle.

"Not too comfortable but I don't think you can ride with that busted leg."

"You do not want to do this," Paco said ominously. Fargo couldn't tell if it was a threat or merely another way of trying to convince him not to return to Fort Davis.

"I don't have much choice. I promise you I won't say a word to the colonel about what you told me, but I will check to see if you're wanted this side of the Rio

Grande. If you are—" Fargo shrugged. "I won't have any choice but to let the colonel know."

"This is rattling my brains and bruising my belly. Let me try to ride. I do not care if there is pain. I have endured it before."

Fargo helped the young man down and then back into the saddle. Paco turned white from the pain as he rode along with his broken, splinted leg stuck out at an impossible angle. But he said nothing.

Fargo walked to the side, the Ovaro's reins in his hand. He watched Paco from the corner of his eye, wondering if he would try to make a run for it.

"You are too honest a man," the vaquero said. "It will be your undoing some day."

"I never found obeying the law to be that hard. Robbing and killing aren't any way to make a living."

"Let me go," Paco ordered. "Let me go and you will be allowed to live."

Fargo laughed. "You've got it backward, friend. I'm the one with the reins and the guns."

The laugh died away when he saw men rising up out of the dark sands all around. He stared down the barrels of at least a dozen pistols and rifles, all cocked and ready to fire at him.

# 12

Fargo saw no way out. He had walked into an ambush because he had been thinking about how to help Paco and had not been paying attention to his surroundings. That failure meant death now.

"You look surprised," spoke up a burly man who came up. He wore bandoliers crossing his chest and six-shooters holstered at either hip. Fargo saw this was the leader of the road agents.

"You're not who I expected," Fargo said. He had thought Frederickson had caught him, but these were Mexicans. Bandidos, from the look of their leader.

Fargo studied him, then turned and stared up at Paco.

"That is right, señor," Paco said. "This is my father."

"Go on, kill him," the man with the bandoliers ordered.

"Stop!" Paco urged the Ovaro forward, putting it between Fargo and the two bandidos lifting their rifles to execute their leader's order. "He saved me. I do not want him harmed."

"He was taking you to the gringo cavalry fort. They would try you and hang you. Or worse. They would turn you over to the Federales."

"He shared his water with me."

"There must be more of a reward for you alive than dead," Paco's father said, shrugging eloquently. "He is like all gringos. A businessman who sees how to squeeze the biggest profit out of any situation."

"I wasn't going to turn him over to Colonel Nolan," Fargo said. "But your son needs medical attention. That

**98**

broken leg might get infected since I don't have the proper medicines."

"We have a *curandera*," the man said.

"Take your son back across the Rio Grande," Fargo said. "If he can get care in Mexico, see to it right away."

"Oh, I will, I will. But first I must kill you. You have seen me, Alfredo the Bandido they call me." The man laughed in delight. Then he turned grim. "Alfredo the Executioner, they ought to call me. I am Alfredo Rodriguez, the most feared bandido in all Chihuahua! You have seen me on this side of the Rio Grande. This will inflame your army, and they will chase me forever."

"I have no fight with you. I'm not a soldier and don't work for them."

"But you know this colonel, eh? You call him by name, so you must have dealings with him. Go on. Shoot him!"

"Father!" cried Paco, but Fargo saw the appeal fell on deaf ears.

"Many men know Colonel Nolan," Fargo said. "Men like Big Red."

"Big Red? Who is this *Rojo Grande*?" Alfredo Rodriguez canted his head to one side, as if sizing up Fargo. This was a change in attitude from the offhand order to shoot him down. Fargo felt a door had opened, and now he must find the right way to go through it to safety.

"The man's name is Frederickson. He knows Nolan better than I do, and they aren't friends. He certainly does not work for the Army."

"That is a good point. You know Frederickson, eh? I would deal with *El Rojo Grande*. Do not shoot him." Alfredo waved his hand, as if he were a king dismissing his subjects. Fargo was grateful that Paco backed up the order with one of his own. The rifles lowered and the fingers left the triggers, but Fargo knew he was still in big trouble. The guns weren't pointed at him, but the circle tightened as Alfredo's men moved closer.

"I know Frederickson," Fargo said.

"And he knows you, eh? *Bueno!*" Alfredo slapped Fargo on the back. A shouted order brought the *ban-*

*didos'* horses from where they had been hidden down in an arroyo.

"My horse!" Paco cried in joy, seeing a strong black stallion being led up by a bandido. The injured man switched horses, leaving Fargo's Ovaro in favor of the big horse. "El Viento!" Paco exclaimed. "I thought never to ride you again. Thank you, Father, for bringing him."

"How'd you find Paco?" Fargo asked, climbing into the saddle so recently abandoned. He had to agree with the bandido leader's son. It was a pleasure being astride a familiar, reliable horse. As fine as El Viento looked, Fargo preferred his own mount.

"I have such a nose," Alfredo said, climbing into a saddle that shone in the night from the silver chasing and conchas mounted on it. The bandido tapped his large nose, then laughed. "I have a big nose, yes, and a good one for the trail. The Federales chased Paco across the river. It was not hard finding where he crossed."

Fargo did not want to know how Alfredo had found out, but he heard anyway.

"I caught the Federales. They did not want to tell me about my son's destination. At first. They told quickly enough after I tortured them. Once on this side of the river, finding Paco was not difficult. This is such an empty land."

"Apaches," Fargo said.

Alfredo laughed. "You have a sense of humor, señor." His mercurial mood shifted again and he said darkly, "Do not allow it to cause your death."

"When can we get home, Father?" Paco asked.

"A day, no longer, my son," Alfredo said. "Come, let us ride!"

The bandidos started riding to the west, but Fargo held back. He had no reason to go with them. He was headed for Fort Davis to tell the colonel about Captain McCall's death, and he had already seen as much of Mexico as he wanted—from this side of the Rio Grande. But Fargo saw he might have to make a detour on his trip to Fort Davis when Alfredo glared at him over his shoulder.

"You will come with us, señor. To Mexico. I must show you proper respect and honor you for saving my favorite son."

"Your only son, Father," Paco called out, enjoying the surge of power from his stallion and rapidly vanishing into the night.

"My only son, yes," Alfredo said. "You will come with us, and I will hold a fiesta in your honor. And while we ride, you must tell me about Frederickson." The way he spoke gave Fargo no chance to decline the bandido's singular accolade.

Fargo wondered what he was getting himself involved in, but seeing no way around it, he rode beside Alfredo and related what he knew of the gunrunner's exploits, to Alfredo's great amusement.

Fargo stared at the raging Rio Grande, tumbling over rocks and churning violently as it raced into a narrow canyon with tumultuous roaring. He shook his head. There was no way they could cross the river into Mexico here.

"Go, go on. Are you afraid?" chided Paco. The man had a smile on his lips that turned into a sneer. "You are afraid. I did not think you would hesitate."

"I almost got washed away at a section of the river where the current wasn't anywhere near as strong," Fargo said. "We should go a mile or two upriver to see if there is a shallow ford."

"He is like an old woman, Paco," said Alfredo. The smile on his face was closer to a leer. Fargo had tired quickly of the bandido's contempt for him. He had no chance to run, and fighting all fifteen of the gang was suicidal, especially after Alfredo had taken his six-shooter and Henry. Whether out of scorn or because he did not notice, the bandido leader let Fargo keep his Arkansas toothpick.

"Perhaps we should show him the way, Father." Paco's stallion reared. He fought to stay on the horse's back, his broken leg flopping at a crazy angle that had to hurt. Paco winced but otherwise showed no pain. To have done so with the rest of the bandidos looking on would have been to lessen his authority. Alfredo and the others respected only strength.

Fargo considered it a false strength. Their machismo would get them killed if they tried fighting the Rio Grande.

"Rio Bravo, we call it," Alfredo said. "We will become like the river, strong and swift and deadly!" With that, he put his spurs to his horse's flanks and shot forward like a Fourth of July rocket. Fargo caught his breath as the bandido plunged into the Rio Grande amid a great splashing of water.

To Fargo's surprise, Alfredo rode fast and straight and his horse did not vanish under the turbulent surface.

"A sandbar?" he asked Paco.

"Go," urged Paco. "Ride fast and do not stop. You will reach the other side."

The Ovaro balked, then obeyed as Fargo sighted on Alfredo on the far side of the river and made a beeline for him. The whirling river rose around the horse's fetlocks but came no higher. As Fargo had guessed, an invisible sandbar provided a shifting but adequate roadway across the river. He splashed up the far bank and stopped beside Alfredo.

After Fargo had seen he and his horse were not going to be washed downriver, he considered his chances of jumping Alfredo before the rest of his men joined them. As he pulled up next to Alfredo, he saw this was a foolish choice.

Alfredo's men were still on the U.S. side of the Rio Grande with Paco—and that did not matter because two dozen more waited for their leader on the Mexican side.

"I lead an army," Alfredo said proudly. "I am a general, and one day I shall be territorial governor. All Coahuila will be mine to run. And Chihuahua. And why stop there? Nuevo Leon and Tamalpais as well! I shall control the entire border from Paso del Norte to Matamoras!"

"That's quite an ambition," Fargo said carefully. "How do you reckon to do this?"

Alfredo fixed sharp eyes on Fargo. "Is that not apparent? The Federales keep me from achieving my rightful position. The politicians are corrupt, thinking only of themselves and enslaving the peasants. No one says, 'We will be better when Alfredo Rey rules over us.'"

"King Alfredo?"

The bandido chief grinned and wheeled his horse around. By the time he rode among his men, Fargo knew it was too late to make a break for it. Not only did Alfredo have enough men to run him down, Paco and the others from the U.S. side were making their way across the river. Alfredo had reunited his men, making a sizable army of thieves.

Fargo rode silently, keeping his eyes peeled and looking for any chance to get away. The longer he stayed with the bandit army, the less hope he had of escaping since they were going deeper into Mexico.

Yet the strain of the past day or two took its toll on Fargo, and he began nodding off as he rode in the hot sun. Only when Alfredo barked an order to dismount did he snap awake.

"It is siesta time," Paco told him. "We sleep until the day is cooler. Do you not find this a fine place to stop?"

Fargo admitted that it was. Jacaranda trees provided adequate shade and a well showed that Alfredo stopped here often enough to make permanent facilities feasible. The bandidos fanned out, some pulling their broad sombreros down right away and going to sleep while others went out on patrol.

"They do not sleep when they are on duty," Paco assured him. "They know what would be done to them."

"Your father heads a strict army," Fargo observed.

"Army, pah," spat Paco. "They are peasants with guns, no more. And many of them do not even have guns. That will change. When we have arms stacked higher than a *cantina,* men will flock to our service. We will see desertion in the Mexican army and gain many trained soldiers."

"Your father told me his plans to rule the entire eastern section of Mexico."

"He is a dreamer," Paco said with some admiration. "He lacks the connections, though. I can provide them."

"You and your father, king and prince of Mexico?"

Paco did not laugh at the idea. If anything, his eyes blazed and a fanatical look came to light his face. Fargo settled back but did not take a siesta with the others. He had fallen in among revolutionaries as well as thieves.

For the moment he was not in any danger. Alfredo had kept him around for some reason, and Paco felt an obligation for the help he had given setting and splinting his leg. Fargo tipped his hat down and leaned back against a tree trunk but kept alert to everything around him. He had thought Paco was going to take a nap, but he hobbled over to his father, talking quietly with three of his lieutenants.

Unable to overhear what they said, Fargo moved closer. He dared not get too close or Alfredo surely would react violently, but Fargo had sharp ears from years on the frontier. Settling down, he strained to eavesdrop—and was glad he did.

His heart beat faster when he heard what Alfredo was saying.

"We will meet soon with him," he said. "This evening El Rojo Grande comes to deal with us."

"How will we pay him, Father?" asked Paco.

"What would a man like Frederickson give for a pardon, eh? He gives us rifles and ammunition, and I grant him a full pardon. He can live on this side of the river and deal with his customers on the other."

"The U.S. will not permit that," Paco protested.

"Let them cross illegally. We will be strong enough to stop them."

"The Federales . . ." one of Alfredo's lieutenants began, only to let the words trail off. Fargo pushed back the brim of his hat and saw the fierce look Alfredo gave the man.

"We will kill them. We will kill them all. They are thieves. They call *us* thieves, but they steal from the peasants. They take all the taxes and give it to a corrupt governor. The peasants will rise up and fight for us if we give them rifles."

"Rifles Frederickson supplies," said Paco.

Fargo listened to the men discussing how to get the weapons from the gunrunner and then not have to pay for them until much later—or ever—and knew he had only a few hours to get away. If Frederickson spotted him, his life was forfeit.

Fargo got up and went off in the direction of a thicket.

"Where are you going?" demanded a guard.

"I have to relieve myself," Fargo said. "I don't see an outhouse anywhere around."

The guard turned and pointed across the encampment. "There's a trench—" As he turned his back on Fargo, the Trailsman moved like a striking snake. His arm circled the guard's throat and tightened until even the last feeble kick died away. Fargo checked. The man was out like a light. A few quick slashes of his knife cut the guard's clothing into strips that Fargo used to bind and gag him. Picking up the fallen rifle, Fargo circled the camp until he came to the horses.

The man guarding the remuda had already joined his amigos in a deep siesta. His snores covering Fargo's cat-step-light approach, the sentry never noticed Fargo take his six-shooter or retrieve his Henry from a stack. So much for the well-disciplined army, Fargo thought. The horses were tired from their morning ride and made little protest as Fargo moved among them and cut out his Ovaro.

He led the horse from camp, heading west into the heart of Mexico. Only when he had gone a half mile did he mount and begin a wide sweeping ride to the north, slanting back toward the Rio Grande and the sanctuary of the United States. As he rode, he used a few simple tricks to hide his trail, but Fargo was more inclined to put as much distance between himself and the bandidos than he was to playing games of subterfuge.

Fargo rode, fearing pursuit, but none came. Either Alfredo's gang could not track competently or the bandido leader considered the missing gringo insignificant compared with dealing with Frederickson for arms. Or perhaps the bound guard had not been found yet. Whatever the reason, Fargo reached the Rio Grande by sundown, crossed, and was back at Fort Davis two days later.

# 13

Fargo dismounted and stretched his tired muscles. He had been keyed up too long and finally arriving at Fort Davis brought all the aches, pains, and tiredness crashing in on him.

"Fargo, you're back?"

"Yes, Colonel, I just couldn't stay away," Fargo said, not bothering to keep the irritation from his voice. He turned to face Colonel Nolan. The man stood with balled hands on his hips, as if he wanted to pick a fight. "Have you heard?"

"Heard what?"

Fargo heaved a deep breath. He had halfway hoped someone else travelling the San Antonio road had come across Captain McCall and had reported it already. From the way Nolan spoke, Fargo knew he was the one bringing the bad news.

"In your office, if you don't mind. This is about Captain McCall and his men."

"Did you overtake them on the road? I told him to send a courier when they reached San Antonio, but no one's come, unless he sent you. That is most irregular."

"Sharp Knife escaped, and McCall and his men are all dead," Fargo said, not wanting to draw out the explanation. The colonel opened his mouth to speak, but nothing came out. Fargo told what had happened and how he had tracked the Apache chief, only to lose him at the Rio Grande a few days earlier.

"You took your time getting back with the news," Nolan accused. "We might have captured the renegades if you had informed me right away."

"I was kidnapped by Mexican bandits," Fargo said. A tiny gasp from behind made him turn. Rachel had one delicate hand over her mouth, her eyes wide in horror.

"Sergeant!" bellowed Nolan. "Find all my officers and assemble them in the mess hall right away. You, Fargo. You will report to my staff so there won't be anything lost by one officer briefing another." Nolan started toward the mess hall, then stopped and in a lower voice said, "Five minutes, Fargo. Five minutes and not one second longer." Nolan glared at Fargo, saluted Rachel, and marched off stiffly.

Fargo saw that the colonel was sweet on Rachel and thought he had competition again. From the way Rachel ran to him and threw her arms around his neck, the colonel might be right.

"Oh, Skye," the young woman cried, holding him close. Her bright blue eyes welled with unshed tears. "I heard. You aren't hurt, are you?"

"No more than I was before I left," he said. He winced when she ran her hand over his head and found some of the lumps he had acquired when he was buffeted around in the Rio Grande after Sharp Knife shot him.

"Oh, no, no more injuries," she said sternly, glaring at him. "I want the post doctor to look at you right away."

"You heard the colonel. He wants me to report to the officers what I've seen. This is important, Rachel."

"More important than dying?"

"I'm all right," he assured her. "Go on back to your quarters. I'll come by when I've finished talking to Nolan and his men."

"If I find you're trying to dodge me, Skye Fargo, you'll wish that horrible Indian chief *had* scalped you!" She tilted her face up to his, saw he was not going to kiss her, so she kissed him. Then she blushed, stepped back, and hurried off holding her skirts just above the dusty parade grounds.

He whistled and caught a private's attention, handed over the Ovaro's reins with a stern admonition to curry and feed the horse, then walked to the mess hall at the rear of the compound. The fort was abuzz, and he knew what they were saying. It had been only minutes since he had told their commander about Captain McCall's death, but everyone knew now. Nothing traveled faster on a military post than bad news.

He stepped into the mess hall and saw a dozen officers seated around the long table with Colonel Nolan at the far end.

"Good, you finally got here," Nolan said brusquely. "Tell the rest of my staff what you told me. Do not leave out any details this time, Fargo." Nolan crossed his arms and glared. Fargo ignored the colonel and launched into a description of how the Apaches had attacked McCall's command and no one survived. He ended with Alfredo's meeting with Big Red Frederickson on the other side of the border.

"Alfredo Rodriguez is no king. He's a petty warlord, a minor bandit chief, and nothing more," Nolan said, dismissing the bandido chieftain's claim to royalty with the wave of his hand. "The Federales have tried unsuccessfully to arrest him for a year or more. We know how corrupt and inefficient they can be. What worries me most is that Frederickson is supplying arms to this scoundrel. Where is he stealing the rifles?"

"Have any shipments been lost recently?" Fargo asked.

"Not to this fort. I'll send a courier to Fort Quitman and Fort Stockton to see if any arms shipments are overdue," Nolan said. The post commander pursed his lips and looked straight at Fargo. "Are you willing to help capture Frederickson?"

"Of course," Fargo said. He owed the gunrunner for his part in killing Ethan Goldman and in kidnapping Rachel. Seeing him convicted in court and hanged would be a pleasure.

"This is not to leave this room. I have been in contact with the Federales, and they are concerned with Frederickson's activities. They had not told me about Alfredo Rodriguez receiving smuggled weapons, but they have mentioned many revolutionaries buying from him. I will send a courier to the *commandante* of the Federales and see if we cannot trap Frederickson before he expands his foul business into Mexico."

"You want me to stay and help with the planning, or can I go get some sleep? I've been in the saddle too long and haven't had time to even eat a proper meal."

"Go on, Mr. Fargo," Nolan said. "I will inform you of your role when we have worked out a plan of capture."

Fargo left, glad to be out of the hot mess hall. Nolan added to the heat with his long harangues, but Fargo had some hope the colonel might capture Frederickson if the U.S. Army worked with the Mexican authorities. He went to the stables and saw that his horse was being properly tended, then went to the barracks where Rachel and her family had been quartered.

To his surprise, they had been moved. Accommodations at Fort Davis were at a premium, and civilians were supposed to move on fast. That Mr. Cleary's injuries had flared up again worried Fargo. He headed for the post surgery and saw Rachel sitting on a step outside the long brick building.

Rachel jumped when he walked up. She had been plucking petals out of a blue wildflower and had not seen him approaching.

"You scared me, Skye."

"Sorry, I didn't mean to. You were mighty intent on destroying that flower."

"I was just thinking."

"About your father? I heard you got moved and he was put back into the hospital."

"Oh, he's doing fine, Skye. I was thinking of other things."

Fargo saw from the way she stared at him what her thoughts were, and that made him uncomfortable. He thought the world of her, but she came from a different background and could never be comfortable on the frontier. She had marrying in mind, and Fargo knew that it would never work out the way she hoped. But she was so lovely and beguiling. Rachel turned to him expectantly.

Her lips parted slightly as her breasts rose and fell faster. He kissed her. Rachel hugged him close. Fargo

**109**

did not intend to go much further. It was best for them both if he ended any affair right now before she got too attached to him.

It was best, but Fargo found Rachel very willing to do more.

Their kiss deepened and tongues darted back and forth, teasing and tormenting and stimulating. Breathing heavily, Rachel pulled back slightly and said in a husky whisper, "I want you, Skye. I know we can never be together forever, but I want you *now*."

"Tomorrow doesn't matter?" he asked.

"Not so much if we make today special." She stroked over his beard and then slid her hand inside his shirt. She moved lower, fingers tightening in his crotch. He sucked in his breath as she started massaging the growing lump she found there.

"Let's go somewhere more private," Fargo said. Together they walked toward the stables. Fargo had seen the soldiers tending the horses leave. He and Rachel could find a soft pile of hay and . . .

She threw herself into his arms and covered him with kisses. As the beautiful dark-haired woman kissed him, her fingers worked on his clothing. His gun belt fell away and then his shirt and trousers. When his erection sprang out, hard and ready, Rachel pounced on it. She lavished more kisses on the tip. Thrills of electric delight blasted into Fargo's loins, and he wanted to give Rachel the same kind of pleasure.

He pulled her close and began lavishing kisses on her lips, ears, face, neck. As he worked lower to a spot between her luxurious breasts, he felt the woman begin to tremble.

"This is so good, Skye, so good," she sobbed out. He moved aside the blouse blocking him from one taut, cherry-sized, nipple. He sucked it into his mouth and felt her begin to shake like a leaf in a high wind. Lapping avidly, he left the rubbery tip in favor of the one capping her left breast. He drew it gently between his lips and tongued it hard. He felt every passionate beat of her heart and knew he had succeeded. He was giving her the same type of arousal she had already given him.

Moving lower proved impossible. Rachel's desires ran wild, and she didn't want more foreplay. She lifted her skirts and fell back on the straw in the stall, legs lifted and spread wide to expose the delightful triangular patch of fleece, already dotted with dew drops, showing her excitement.

"Hurry, Skye. Don't be gentle. Don't hold back. I need you so much!" She lifted her knees, rocked back and waited for him. He felt the same urgency and moved quickly. His shaft brushed across her nether lips and then parted them. For a moment he hung suspended between earth and heaven.

Then he found paradise. He shoved forward and sank all the way into her womanly depths. Rachel gasped. The shudder passed from her body down lower. Fargo thought she was going to crush him flat. It felt as if a sensuous velvet glove gripped him and refused to let go. Rotating his hips, stirring around inside her tightness, gave them both added enjoyment before he pulled back slowly.

A lewd sucking sound filled the stables as he slipped from her gripping pit. Rachel's eyes fluttered open and she looked panicked, as if he was going to stop. Before she could say a word, Fargo positioned himself again and plunged forward. She had asked for it hard and fast. He gave it to her.

Friction built along the length of his fleshy column, burning him and igniting Rachel's sexual cravings to the point of no return. She thrashed about under him, pinioned by the hardness of his manhood. The dark-haired beauty began kicking out and then drawing her legs back up tight against her body. This tightened and relaxed the female sheath surrounding him and made it more difficult for Fargo to keep control.

He wanted this to last forever, but everything Rachel did—everything he did—robbed him of his iron will. He was aflame inside. Her carnal heat burned at him delightfully, and every stroke caused the woman to cry out in joy. He sped up, moving faster and faster until he lost all sense of himself.

He heard Rachel cry out in utter ecstasy, but it was

distant, far away, on some other world. Fargo knew what a mountain felt before an avalanche. The expectation, the tension, the utter exhilaration of release. Pumping fiercely, he drove back and forth until he exploded and then turned flaccid within the woman's clinging tightness. Fargo sagged down, stared into the woman's sex-blurred eyes, and then kissed her.

"Oh, Skye, that was *so* good," she sighed. She reached up and pulled him down. They kissed some more, but the rush of passion had left them both sated.

For a time.

Fargo finally said, "I've got to see what the colonel has cooked up."

"You're leaving again?"

He nodded. "Nolan has an alliance with the Federales across the border. He figures to capture Frederickson to cut off the flow of contraband."

"You don't sound happy about it, Skye. Why not?"

"I want Frederickson to stand trial for all he did to you, but Sharp Knife is the one who has to be stopped. He'll keep inciting the Apaches to raid. There's no telling how many more will die if he isn't returned to the reservation where the Army can watch him."

"He ought to be in jail." Rachel shook as if she had developed a chill. "But let the cavalry handle this, Skye. It's not your job to bring all the outlaws to justice."

"It might not be my job," Fargo said, "but I'm going to do what I can. This is personal." And for him it was. No amount of time in prison—or even a noose—could repay the debt Big Red Frederickson had racked up. And Sharp Knife led a band of bloodthirsty renegades likely to kill everyone they came across unless he was stopped.

"I thought you'd say that. It's the way you are." Rachel laid her head on his chest. He felt hot tears on his bare skin and didn't know what to say to comfort her. If there was anything he could do at all.

"The trap is set and baited," Colonel Nolan said with some satisfaction. Fargo had followed Nolan and his soldiers to an overlook along the river. "The bandidos on

112

the Mexican side of the Rio Grande will cross the river to where we nab them when the Federales attack. And if Rodriguez and his men don't try to escape, then the Mexican authorities have made quite a haul today."

"Frederickson will go across at the ford?" Fargo asked, looking down from the canyon rim to the raging river below.

"This is the only place within miles he can come back. When he sees the Federales attack, he'll come right back across and we'll be waiting to capture him."

"Not a bad plan," Fargo said, worrying that Nolan had missed a detail or two along the way. Alfredo's men raided throughout this part of the river and intimately knew every bend and shallow in the river. From what Fargo had heard about the Mexican army, they lacked training and discipline and might even be in Alfredo's employ. The trap would never be sprung if one of the poorly paid Federales told Alfredo.

He shrugged it off. This was his best chance at capturing the gunrunner and his men. Alfredo—and Paco—were outlaws but had done nothing to Fargo, and he was content to let the Mexican authorities deal with them.

"There, there he is," Nolan said excitedly.

Fargo saw Frederickson and a half dozen of his men making their way down the riverbank, leading a pack train of mules laden with long boxes.

"Did you hear where he stole the rifles?" Fargo asked. "There must be fifty rifles there."

"The Fort Quitman armorer might have sold them to him. Major Lawson found more than a hundred rifles missing. Look, there, Fargo, there! He's crossing the river. Get ready."

The order went out to Colonel Nolan's men. The cavalry troopers mounted their mules and prepared to make their way down the winding path on the cliff face. Fargo thought this was the most dangerous part of the attempted capture, since a sniper on the far side of the river could take potshots at them as they negotiated the hairpin bends in the trail.

As dangerous as it was, Fargo started down first. He wanted to be sure Frederickson did not get away.

Now and then he cast a glance down at the raging river. Frederickson crossed at the sandbar and had reached the far side of the river to greet Alfredo when the Federales attacked prematurely. They should have waited until the rifle-laden mules had crossed, but they came riding into Alfredo's camp, sabers flashing and guns blazing.

"He's coming back across," Fargo called to Colonel Nolan a dozen feet behind him. "They should have waited until we were down at the river."

Fargo heard Nolan cursing but could make no sense of it. The colonel cried out orders that could never be executed while they were stranded along the narrow, winding trail. Fargo urged his sure-footed Ovaro down faster. The horse kicked loose more stones and slipped now and then, but Fargo felt the need to reach the river.

Frederickson got back to the U.S. side long minutes before Fargo got off the trail. The gunrunner drew his pistol and sent a few slugs flying in Fargo's direction, but the intent was to slow pursuit rather than to kill.

Fargo found himself on the horns of a dilemma. It would take Nolan's men some time to reach the bottom of the trail and form an effective line. He could go after the fleeing Frederickson or he could stop the rest of the gunrunners from crossing the Rio Grande.

The leader or the half dozen others responsible for the illicit trade?

Fargo drew his Henry, aimed at Frederickson's rapidly disappearing back, and knew he had no shot. He turned to the men in the middle of the river struggling to escape the Federales. A shot took out one man. A second shot caused another's horse to rear and impede the progress of the others. This forced the gunrunners to stop and decide whether to push ahead into Fargo's deadly fire or to take their chances with Alfredo against the Federales.

Seeing he had slowed them enough for Nolan to get his men lined up and ready to fight, Fargo took off after Frederickson. The cavalry troopers, except Nolan and his officers, were all mounted on mules and could never catch up with the escaping outlaw. Fargo's Ovaro flew alongside the churning, roiling Rio Grande. He put his head down and cradled the Henry rifle in front of him as he pursued Big Red Frederickson.

The gunrunner had lit out but had not gotten far enough to elude Fargo. Within two miles Fargo narrowed the gap between them. When Frederickson's horse began to tire, Fargo knew he had him.

"Give up, Frederickson. Give up or I'll cut you down." Fargo shot at the outlaw and missed only because Frederickson's horse stumbled and almost threw its rider. The horse regained its balance, but Fargo was even closer.

"I don't want to hang. Better to take a bullet in the gut!" Frederickson began shooting, but Fargo was already galloping flat-out toward the man. When Frederickson's six-shooter came up empty, Fargo knew he had him.

As he rushed past, Fargo swung his rifle. The barrel caught the gunrunner on the side of the head and knocked him off his horse. The horse stood for a moment, then realized its punishing rider was gone. It bolted, leaving Frederickson on the ground with Fargo towering over him.

Fargo levered another round into the Henry and pointed it at the outlaw.

"Give up, Frederickson, give up."

Big Red Frederickson dropped his empty six-gun and slowly lifted his hands in surrender.

## 14

Fargo walked the gunrunner back to where Colonel Nolan was finishing the short but fierce fight as the Mexican bandidos tried to follow Frederickson across the Rio Grande. Alfredo, Paco, and a half dozen of their men stood in a tight clump, muttering among themselves. The bandido leader looked up when he saw Fargo returning with Frederickson in custody.

"You, I should have killed you." Alfredo Rodriguez turned and cuffed Paco. "You are a fool. A man saving your life does not mean he is your friend!" He started to hit his son again, but one of Nolan's men prevented it.

"You shouldn't hold up people and buy illegal arms from gunrunners," Fargo told Alfredo. The man's swarthy face clouded over, and he spat at Fargo. The spittle caught·on the wind and vanished over the river.

"I will kill you! I will cut out your tongue and roast you in the hot sun and make you wish Apaches had captured you!" screamed Alfredo. He pushed his son away when Paco tried to calm him. "You will learn to fear every sound behind you. It will be me coming for you!"

Fargo laughed and shook his head. Even an Apache would have a devil of a time sneaking up on him. A loud, blundering bandido more used to riding a powerful stallion than stalking his quarry stood no chance of bringing down the Trailsman.

"Shut up, you," Colonel Nolan said. He waved to a Mexican officer on the far side of the river. The Federale carefully picked his way across, a squad of soldiers trailing him.

*"Mi coronel!"* greeted the Federale. "You have snared these bandidos for me."

"Take them, General Paloma," Nolan said, pointing at Alfredo and his men. "Send me news of how their trials turn out."

"Oh, they will be found guilty. Make no mistake. They will be given a fair trial and then hanged!" The Mexican general laughed, then motioned for his men to herd Alfredo and the others back to the far side of the Rio Grande. "You will hear from the governor, who will certainly give you his sincere thanks for this." The general paused and pointed at Frederickson. "What of that one? He came into my country to sell illegal arms."

Fargo heard a longing note in the Mexican officer's voice, as if he wanted what Frederickson was selling. From the expression of hope that flared on the gunrunner's face, Fargo knew it would be tantamount to releasing Frederickson if they turned him over to the Federales. To his relief, Fargo saw that Colonel Nolan recognized this also.

"We want him for too many crimes to mention. He committed one against your country. Against mine, who can count that high? He must pay. In the U.S."

General Paloma shrugged, then followed his men with their prisoners back to the Mexican side of the river.

"Your luck just ran out, Frederickson," Fargo said.

"Yeah. Even worse, that Mexican bandido is going to keep my rifles."

"Alfredo?"

Frederickson shook his head. "Paloma. You don't think he's going to return them or the mules, do you?"

Fargo looked at Nolan, who seemed caught up in a moral dilemma about demanding that Paloma return the rifles, since they had been pilfered from Fort Quitman, or simply letting the Mexican general go on his way.

"Maybe he can use the rifles, Colonel," Fargo said. "The banditos were better armed than the Federales."

"He'll probably sell them himself," grumbled Nolan. He came to a decision, pushed recovering the rifles from his mind, and formed his men into columns for the trip back to Fort Davis with Frederickson and four of his henchmen in custody.

As pleased as Colonel Nolan was, Fargo was less than happy with the outcome. Frederickson might be out of the picture, but Sharp Knife was still raiding throughout West Texas. Until the Apache chief was stopped, Fargo could not rest easy.


"I don't want to go, but Papa's insisting," Rachel said. She sat close to Fargo under the canopy outside the Fort Davis hospital, hands folded in her lap. "He looked over La Limpia, he said, and decided there wasn't enough for us here."

"So he wants to push on to Franklin?"

"He thinks Fort Bliss at Magoffinsville is a better place for us. With Franklin close by, and the Butterfield stage going into Hueco Tanks, the number of people within a day's ride will make us rich."

"Not from a seed store," Fargo said.

"He wants to set up a general store. We can get supplies from San Antonio and sell to Post El Paso, Fort Fillmore, even across the Rio Grande to people from Paso del Norte. One day, Papa says, the railroad will come through the pass and make the area incredibly important."

"That'll be years and years," Fargo said. He knew Rachel was only telling him this so he would try to talk her out of going with her family. He didn't try dissuading her because she had no real choice but to go. Staying with him was wrong, and they both knew it. Rachel was just a little slow admitting it to herself.

Fargo listened with half an ear as she went on about Fort Bliss. He held his breath, then let it out slowly because an idea was coming to him. It was dangerous and not one he wanted to mention aloud, but it might be their best chance at flushing out Sharp Knife and his Apache renegades. Sharp Knife had a special taste for settlers and their wagons. He might be enticed to attack the Cleary family again if he thought they were traveling unguarded from Fort Stockton northwest to Fort Bliss.

It posed an immense danger for Rachel and the rest

of her family, and considering all they had been through, it might be beyond their ability to endure. But having them on the trail would be dangerous no matter what, like dangling a fish in front of a cat. Sharp Knife would find them a delectable—and irresistible—attraction.

Fargo justified it by reasoning that he would be able to protect them himself. Colonel Nolan and his troopers were seasoned veterans, but their record against Sharp Knife was not good.

Fargo snorted and shook his head, recollecting how *his* record against the Apache chief wasn't so stellar, either. The Apache renegade had left him for dead in the Rio Grande. Fargo had quite a score to settle with him. And he would. Using the Cleary family as bait.

"Come with me," he told Rachel. "I want to talk with your pa to see if he'll go along with an idea that just came to me."

Rachel opened her mouth to say something, but Fargo already had her by the elbow and was guiding her toward the post infirmary to discuss the matter of a full military escort from Fort Davis to Fort Bliss—along with a trap set to capture Sharp Knife.

"There's no reason to be so antsy, Fargo," Colonel Nolan said. "That was a right good plan you concocted."

Fargo wasn't so sure now that they were putting it into effect. The Cleary family was split between two wagons, neither fully loaded with their belongings and both with a half dozen hidden soldiers in the rear. Rachel's brothers, Abel and Joshua, drove one wagon and her father the other, though he required Rachel's help in getting the mules moving. Fargo had wanted to ride with Rachel, but Nolan had dissuaded him.

"There's no telling what Sharp Knife would do if he saw you. He'd certainly suspect a trap," the colonel had said. And Fargo had agreed.

"The camels," Fargo asked. "Are they within striking distance?"

"The camels move a lot faster than horses across this terrain. Old Jeff Davis had himself a good idea bringing them in." Nolan cleared his throat and added, "Well, mostly a good idea. They are about as mean and cantankerous an animal as I ever laid eyes on."

Fargo knew of the camels' temperament and worried more about Rachel's safety. Her father was on the mend but hardly in condition to do any serious fighting. Her mother was better off but not fully healed, either. He wanted to be in the wagon with the hidden soldiers. That wasn't feasible, and both he and Nolan knew the reason.

Should anything go wrong and Sharp Knife not be captured, Fargo had to be in a position to hunt the renegade down.

"You want to ride ahead and scout?" Nolan asked, wanting to be rid of Fargo.

"I'll stick with the main body of soldiers," Fargo said. About half the troopers rode horses or camels. The rest sat astride the sure-footed, slow-moving mules. Should the soldiers be killed, getting to the Cleary party would take precious time. Fargo knew that he could ride quickest to the danger before them.

"I told Mr. Cleary to follow the Butterfield road. If Sharp Knife is out hunting for something to raid, he won't be far away. The sight of two wagons driven by civilians will be more than he can pass up."

"If he's in the area," Fargo said. But in his gut he knew Sharp Knife was here. He felt the war chief's presence as surely as he did the hot sun burning on his back.

Against Fargo's advice, the Clearys kept moving through the day, enduring the heat and working their way slowly to the northwest along the stagecoach road. The desert provided any number of good spots for an ambush, and Fargo dreaded seeing the wagons go down into the depressions because he might not see them come out on the far rim.

Just before the worst heat of the day, around five o'clock, Fargo perked up. His sensitive ears had heard something none of the others had. The soldiers were riding along, heads bowed and dozing in the saddles. Their horses and mules walked along slowly, and the camels were hidden a couple miles to the right of the road. Fargo sat straighter and scanned the horizon. The wagons strained up an incline to get out of a sun-baked dried mud flat. This was the perfect spot for an ambush, since they could never hope to get up any speed to escape.

"Colonel!" Fargo cried. "Ahead!"

He put his heels to the Ovaro's flanks and shot forward. The heat struck him in the face as if he had opened a blast furnace door. Fargo put his head down and coaxed more speed from his horse. The heat worked against them, but speed was necessary if he wanted to protect Rachel and her family.

The first gunshots sounded almost a minute after Fargo had given the colonel warning. Through the heat haze Fargo saw the soldiers in the wagons methodically firing at the Apaches attacking them. The Indians had been caught by surprise and a half dozen lay dead on the ground. Another dozen whooped and hollered and circled the wagons.

Fargo glanced to his right and saw brown dots appearing—the camels under Corporal Williams's command. They were coming fast across the hot West Texas sands, but Fargo would reach the wagons first.

As he rode, he studied the Apaches to identify their leader. Sharp Knife had eagle feathers in his black hair and wore distinctive war paint. Fargo ignored the other Apaches and rode toward the war chief.

Sharp Knife spotted him and got off several rounds in his direction. Fargo bent low and kept riding. The Apache chief screamed orders and waved his rifle high over his head. Fargo wanted to cry out to the soldiers in the backs of the wagons not to shoot him, that Sharp Knife was *his*. But his cries would be drowned out as volley after volley cut through the attacking renegades.

Fargo single-mindedly rode for Sharp Knife, but another saw him as an easy target. A war club whistled past the side of his head, barely missing him. The Ovaro missed a step, staggered and then recovered, wheeling around. Fargo had no choice but to deal with his attacker.

He slid his six-shooter from its holster and fired point-blank. The bullet caught the Apache in the shoulder and knocked him from his horse. The warrior jumped to his feet, but his right arm hung uselessly at his side. Grabbing for his knife with his left hand, the Apache would have continued the fight, but he looked up into the barrel of Fargo's six-gun.

"Surrender," Fargo ordered. The Indian hesitated, considering his chances, then sullenly dropped his knife and raised his good hand.

"See to him," Fargo called to a soldier in the rear of the wagon Abel Cleary had driven. All around lay the bodies of dead Apaches, and more were throwing down their rifles and knives, surrendering rather than being cut down.

Fargo galloped in a full circle around the wagons, hunting for Sharp Knife, but he didn't see the Apache chief.

"Skye!" called Rachel, waving to him. "Skye!"

He trotted over. "You all right? You and the rest of your family?"

"That was him, wasn't it? That terrible savage with the war paint."

"That was Sharp Knife," he confirmed. Fargo saw that Rachel and the others were unharmed, wisely having taken cover in the rear of the wagon at the first sign of danger. The soldiers had executed their defense perfectly, waiting long enough before firing to draw in the Apaches but putting up a spirited fight once they had engaged.

"We got them, Fargo, we got them!" gloated Colonel Nolan, riding up. Fargo saw Corporal Williams and his half dozen camel corpsmen arriving at last.

"All but one, Colonel," Fargo said grimly. "Sharp Knife got away. For the time being."

Fargo looked west, into the worst of the West Texas desert, and knew Sharp Knife had escaped in that direction. There were no visible tracks in the shifting sands, and the heat masked any movement all the way to the horizon, but Fargo knew Sharp Knife had gone that way.

With a nod in Rachel's direction and a shout of encouragement to Corporal Williams, Fargo started after Sharp Knife. This time the Apache would not get away.

# 15

The country was entirely different from the rocky banks of the Rio Grande, where Sharp Knife had ambushed him before. Fargo pulled his hat down lower to shield his face, but blocking out the sun was not all he needed to do if he wanted to protect himself. The hot wind gusting across the sandy, rocky terrain slashed at his flesh like a knife. Fargo could feel the moisture being sucked from his body.

Squinting, he tried to find Sharp Knife's trail. The wily Apache chief had lit out, making no attempt to hide his tracks. That changed within a mile of where the cavalry ambush had succeeded so brilliantly.

"Just you and me," Fargo said, pulling up his bandanna to keep grit from getting into his mouth. He looked like a bandit and felt like a lawman. This time he was not going to give up hunting Sharp Knife. One of them might die. They both might die. But Fargo was not giving up until Sharp Knife's threat to West Texas was eliminated.

It had become personal. That might be clouding his judgment, and he knew it, so he worked to be as level-headed as possible.

Sharp Knife's tracks vanished in the shifting sand and forced Fargo to rely on his frontier sense. He followed the contours in the desert where they took him, as a fleeing Apache might go, then, following his instincts, he cut northeast toward San Angelo.

Fargo smiled when he saw the Indian's knife on the sands. He dismounted and gingerly picked it up. Thoughts of using Sharp Knife's own knife against him ran through Fargo's head, but then he cast the blade away. The horn handle had broken, leaving behind the metal blade and shaft. Until the haft was replaced, the knife wasn't worth spit. What finding the blade did for Fargo, though, was convince him his skills were sharp as ever. He was definitely on Sharp Knife's scent.

Fargo walked his Ovaro a while and then mounted when the animal began rearing and pawing at the air. Fargo wanted to see what was exciting the horse. Less than a mile farther he saw the source of the horse's agitation. A small watering hole surrounded by cottonwoods. It looked like paradise, but Fargo held the horse in check, not daring to run pell-mell for the water until he knew Sharp Knife was not laying a trap for him.

He circled the watering hole, hunting for any sign of the Apache chief. As far as he could tell, Sharp Knife had never even come to this water source. That struck Fargo as odd, since the Mescalero had been making a beeline for this spot. Drawing his six-shooter, Fargo jumped to the ground and gave his Ovaro its head. The horse trotted for the water, leaving its rider behind.

Fargo followed warily—and with good reason. Sharp Knife had set a trap for him. If Fargo had ridden in, he would have been shot out of the saddle. As it was, Sharp Knife came from hiding to see why the Ovaro was riderless, giving Fargo his chance to cock his six-gun, aim, and fire. The range was too long for a good shot and he missed.

The Apache chief whirled around, startled. Fargo saw the mask of hatred on the man's face. Sharp Knife let out a screech and followed it with a war whoop as he charged. The Indian fired his rifle at Fargo but made little effort to aim. The hot lead whistled past, missing by a foot or more.

Fargo gauged his distance and took more careful aim, winging Sharp Knife. The wound wasn't enough to slow the Mescalero's attack. Fargo aimed again and squeezed, intending this to be a killing shot. His six-shooter jammed. And then Sharp Knife leapt, and he found himself all wrapped up in a straining, kicking, fighting Apache intent on choking him to death.

Sharp Knife fought with maniacal fury. Fargo was bowled over by the intensity but fought more rationally. He had avoided the Apache's ambush, and that had infuriated Sharp Knife. But Fargo could only be cool and calculating so long. This was a fight for his life. He grabbed Sharp Knife's brawny wrists and twisted hard, throwing the chief to one side. This gave Fargo the chance to run his forearm across the Indian's throat, choking him from behind.

Sharp Knife kicked and thrashed and then got his foot against the rough trunk of a cottonwood. Using the leverage, he shoved back hard and landed on top of Fargo, momentarily stunning him. As Fargo's iron-bar lock across Sharp Knife's throat eased, the Apache twisted savagely and got free.

"I will kill you," Sharp Knife said, panting harshly, spittle spraying with each word. He drew another knife, one that gleamed in the bright sunlight. The war chief twisted it from side to side so the reflection crossed Fargo's lake-blue eyes, blinding him intermittently.

"Let's do this right," Fargo said, drawing his Arkansas toothpick. "To the death!"

Sharp Knife lunged, slashing for Fargo's face to force him to recoil. Fargo dodged and attacked rather than retreating. He drove his knife forward, trying to sink it into the Indian's belly. Somehow, Sharp Knife managed to avoid what should have been a killing stroke. They locked together again, left hands clamped around knife wrists, muscles straining and legs driving forward to gain advantage. Fargo felt his grip slipping as the hot sun greased their hands with sweat.

They held immobile for a moment, then Sharp Knife sidestepped and Fargo lost his balance. He fell heavily, rolled, and came to his feet in the slick mud of the watering hole. Fargo lunged clumsily, using his long-bladed Arkansas toothpick as a shield to keep the Apache at bay.

Sharp Knife crashed into him again, and the two of them fell heavily in the middle of the water. A crazy thought flashed through Fargo's brain. He might drown in the middle of one of the worst deserts in the country.

125

Face underwater, he fought to get a breath. Sharp Knife was determined to hold him under.

With a kick and a twist, Fargo toppled Sharp Knife and returned the favor, trying to drown his adversary. The Apache surged, lifted Fargo high in the air, and dropped him. He landed hard. Stunned, Fargo fought to keep his knife in front of him and keep a grip on consciousness. Sputtering, fighting, thrashing around in the water, he finally got to his knees. The water was blinding him. With a quick wipe he got the water off his face and looked around to find Sharp Knife.

The Apache chief was nowhere to be seen.

"Sharp Knife!" he shouted. Furious, Fargo got to his feet and slogged out of the muddy watering hole. "Sharp Knife! Get back here and fight like a man!"

For whatever reason, the Apache had hightailed it, leaving Fargo and his rage behind. That anger grew when Fargo saw how the Ovaro had kept drinking from the watering hole throughout the fight. Already the horse's belly was distended and growing as the horse continued to drink.

"Get away from there," Fargo said, tugging on the bridle to get the horse away from the water. He patted the horse's flanks and saw the bloating wasn't too extreme, but he wasn't going to get on and ride any time soon. He had to wait for the water to work its way through the animal. If he tried riding the Ovaro in this condition, it might up and die under him.

"Damn you, Sharp Knife!" Fargo raged. Then he settled down in the shade of a cottonwood to wait. He reckoned the bloating would go down by dusk, and he could get back after Sharp Knife.

The starlight was bright enough for Fargo to track Sharp Knife. The enforced rest back at the watering hole had done much to restore Fargo's vitality and fired his determination to bring in the Apache renegade. The Ovaro seemed none the worse for its bout of bloating, but Fargo kept the pace slow, as much out of concern for his horse as to avoid any new trap Sharp Knife might lay.

Now and then Fargo studied the stars to get his bearings. The Milky Way arched high and luminous in the West Texas sky, giving him a better sense of direction than the North Star. As he rode, he wondered if Sharp Knife was trying to lead him in circles. The Apache's trail curved around to the northwest and eventually led back west, as if he was trying once more to escape across the Rio Grande.

That might be the chief's intention, but as Fargo rode he thought harder on other, more aggressive destinations. Fargo urged his horse to greater speed as certainty settled on him. Sharp Knife was not trying to merely escape. He wanted revenge and knew how to take it on Fargo without fighting hand-to-hand again.

"Rachel," Fargo said. He had no idea where the Cleary family had gone after the successful ambush, but he doubted Mr. Cleary wanted to return to Fort Davis. It had been too easy convincing the man to go along with setting the trap because he had taken it into his head to establish his store at Fort Bliss rather than the smaller town of La Limpia near Fort Davis.

Colonel Nolan would return to Fort Davis with his prisoners, and the Clearys would drive on along the Butterfield stage route toward Hueco Tanks and eventually Fort Bliss. And they would be riding unprotected because Nolan would not want to send along a detachment when he thought the Apache danger was past.

Fargo wondered if Sharp Knife had come to the same conclusions about what Nolan and Cleary would do or if there was some sixth sense the Apache relied on to cause devilment. The Apache chief seemed to know instinctively how to create the most chaos.

Fargo rode a little faster, less concerned with the trail than in reaching the Butterfield road.

He couldn't believe it was barely a day since the cavalry had sprung the trap and eliminated most of Sharp Knife's renegade band. Fargo wiped sweat off his forehead and looked up and down the road with its double ruts cut into the hard ground. He could not tell if the Clearys had pushed on north or if they had even passed this way. The ground was as hard as rock and bore no imprint.

"North," Fargo said to himself. "Cleary will want to get away from Fort Davis as fast as he can." He turned his Ovaro to the north and started riding, slowly at first and then with a greater sense of purpose. Fargo saw nothing to confirm the Cleary wagon had rolled this way, but deep in his gut he knew it was true. There were no traces of horses or camels to suggest the cavalry had gone along as protection, but when he found a pile of barely dry mule scat he knew he had guessed right.

Occasionally reaching the top of a dusty hill or the rim of a large sun-baked bowl gave him the chance to look ahead along the road. It meandered around hills and seemed to have no rhyme or reason to it. Knowing the Butterfield surveyor had simply told the stagecoach drivers which places to avoid as opposed to places to drive gave Fargo a sense of how the road followed the burning contours of the West Texas landscape.

He rode until he wondered where the next stage way station would be. The Clearys ought to have found it by now, with some sweet water and the chance to talk to a stationmaster half crazy with loneliness and heat. Fargo topped another steep rise and saw the wagon ahead.

His heart leapt—and then caught in his throat. He had been right about everything. The Clearys had continued along the road on their way to Fort Bliss. Sharp Knife had also taken out after them, intent on revenge. The wagon was canted to one side, as it had been the first time Fargo had seen it.

The difference between the two events was startling. Before, the Apache band had circled them as they returned fire. This time only Sharp Knife was coming after them, and no one in the wagon knew it.

The Apache chief rode up an arroyo parallel to the deeply rutted path. He stopped now and then and poked his head up as if he could see over the rim of the deeply cut gully, then went farther, intending to attack from the side where he was less likely to be spotted until it was too late for the settlers to fight back.

Fargo reached for his Henry, then stopped. The

Clearys needed help again, but he did not think their plight was as bad as before. If he captured Sharp Knife, they would be safer for it. Colonel Nolan would have given them adequate water and supplies, so they could endure the burning heat for a few days.

If he was successful in capturing Sharp Knife, they would only have to survive for the next few minutes.

Fargo judged the attack that would give him the best chance of ending Sharp Knife's threat and figured trailing the Apache chief down the arroyo would bag the renegade with the least danger. He urged his Ovaro down the crumbling embankment into the gravel-bottomed arroyo. Safely down the treacherous, sandy slope, Fargo pulled his Henry from its saddle scabbard and then rode forward at a brisk walk. The Ovaro's hooves crunched on the dry bed, but Sharp Knife paid no attention. He was watching his victims, intent on his attack.

When the Indian chief found a break in the arroyo bank and started up, Fargo leveled his rifle, aimed, and fired.

The dull thwat! of the hammer hitting the primer and lack of recoil told him he had a hang-fire. He quickly ejected the faulty cartridge and aimed again—only to find empty desert in his sights. Cursing, he galloped forward to the spot where Sharp Knife had left the arroyo to mount his attack.

The chief made not a sound as he advanced on the hapless wagon. Mr. Cleary and his two sons fought to get the wagon upright so they could work on the back wheel, the same one that had given them trouble before.

Fargo took in everything in a flash. The Clearys. Sharp Knife. The distance. The impossible shot required to stop the attack.

Fargo lifted his rifle and began firing as smoothly as he could, sending out a fan of hot lead in the faint hope of hitting Sharp Knife. The range was too great, but the firing accomplished another of his goals. The men looked up and saw Sharp Knife charging toward them.

The boys dived under the wagon, shouting to their mother and sister. Mr. Cleary grabbed for the long-barreled shotgun Abel had been so insistent on carrying. He hefted it and discharged it before he had a good bead on Sharp Knife.

The goose gun barked and sent its heavy load of shot to the attacking Indian's left. Sharp Knife ducked low and started firing with a six-shooter. Mr. Cleary jerked and dropped the shotgun, provoking a cry of fear from Joshua. The younger boy scrambled from under the disabled wagon and scooped up the shotgun. He tried to fire it, but Sharp Knife was too close. The Apache had emptied his gun but bent low and swung, hitting Joshua in the head with the six-shooter's barrel. The boy fell back, bounced off the wagon, and then lay facedown in the dust.

Sharp Knife let out a wild whoop of triumph, turned, and gestured angrily at Fargo. The Trailsman lifted his rifle but did not take the shot. If he missed, he might hit Rachel, who now stood in the driver's box behind Sharp Knife.

The Apache took this as a sign of weakness on Fargo's part, laughed, and then galloped away. He had won. He had attacked the wagon and brought down two of the men before racing off.

Fargo looked from the Cleary wagon to the dust cloud Sharp Knife's pony was kicking up in his headlong retreat. He wasn't sure his tired horse could outrun Sharp Knife's. He wasn't even sure if he could get the Ovaro into a gallop until it rested.

He lowered his rifle and went to see how badly injured the Clearys were. Sharp Knife would take it as a weakness on his part, but Fargo knew where his duty lay. When the settlers were safe, he would be back on Sharp Knife's trail.

The renegade Apache *would* find justice at the hands of the Trailsman.

## 16

"Is he all right?" Fargo asked, dismounting. He hurried to kneel beside Joshua. The boy was still out like a light. Mr. Cleary held his son, but he was in almost as bad shape.

"I don't know," Mr. Cleary said, gritting his teeth in pain.

"You sit and rest," Fargo said, giving the man a once-over. He didn't see any blood, but from the way Cleary moved, he might have wrenched something inside.

"He's my son!"

"I don't want to see him die any more than you," Fargo said. He put his hand on Joshua's forehead. Although sweating, he seemed normal enough. Fargo had seen more than one man who had been conked on the head turn pale and clammy, then pass out. Their temperature dropped like a stone and their eyes unfocused. Prying open Joshua's eyelids didn't tell Fargo much, but it calmed the Clearys. They assumed he knew exactly what he was doing.

Gently probing, Fargo found a goose egg–sized lump on the back of the boy's head. He had fallen and struck his head on the side of the wagon. As Fargo pressed into the softness, Joshua moaned softly. A good sign.

"What can we do, Skye?"

Fargo looked up at Rachel.

"We have to be real careful about moving him," he told her. "Fixing the wagon is the first thing to do so we can get you back to Fort Davis."

"We're going on to Fort Bliss," protested Cleary. "That would mean backtracking two or more days."

"More, unless I miss my guess," Fargo said, his mind racing. He dared not leave them, yet he felt Sharp Knife getting away from him. He took it personally that the Apache chief had succeeded in raiding and bedeviling the Clearys while he did nothing. The two of them had a personal, private fight in progress, and letting Sharp Knife escape now only prolonged their final meeting.

He wanted Sharp Knife brought to justice, but he knew the Apache chief might prefer their duel being to the death. Fargo wanted to keep the Mescalero from taking anyone else along with him if their trail came to that sorry end.

"Will he die if we don't go back?"

"I know there's a doctor at Fort Davis," Fargo said. "He patched you—and me—up pretty good and is likely to have seen this kind of injury before. More than one recruit's taken a header off his horse and landed head down."

"Very well," Cleary said, as if he was making the decision. "We will go back. Rachel, keep your brother's lips damp. Dribble a little water onto them by wringing out a wet cloth."

Fargo stood and got a good look at the wagon. When he had found them weeks ago on the road between Fort Stockton and Fort Davis the wheel had come free because the hub had loosened. The time spent at Fort Davis had not gone to repairing the wagon. The same problem had caused this minor disaster.

Fargo looked around and was not surprised when he saw nothing to use as a lever to lift the wagon. Wood of any kind, much less a branch six feet or more long and hefty enough to use without breaking, was a rarity.

"I'll get the wagon lifted as much as I can. You help out, Abel. Put a rock under the axle when we lift. It'll take some work, but we can do it inch by inch."

"I'll help," Cleary offered. Pain washed over his face and turned him white.

"You bust a rib?"

"Might have," he allowed.

"Then Rachel can help us lift. Her and your missus,

too, while you stack the rocks. After we get some of the load taken out."

It was early the next day before they had jacked up the wagon enough so Fargo could slide on the wagon wheel. They were all exhausted from their work, and he was especially disheartened. The Cleary family was safe and the trip back to Fort Davis would be as uneventful as it was slow, to keep from jostling Joshua around too much. But every day, every second, spent not trailing Sharp Knife meant the shrewd Mescalero chief had time to run, to hide, to recruit more Apaches off the reservation. Fargo did not want to think about what mischief Sharp Knife had brewing.

"Get Joshua cushioned the best you can," Fargo said, helping Rachel and Abel lift their brother into the wagon bed. "That mattress will do fine to take up some of the jolting." He worried that the boy had not regained full consciousness since he had bumped his head. Joshua took water and a little food, as long as it was soft, and he groaned occasionally, but other than these favorable signs he simply lay like a corpse.

Fargo whipped the reins of his Ovaro around a ring mounted at the rear of the wagon, then climbed into the driver's box.

"I can drive," Mr. Cleary said testily.

"I know you can," Fargo said, "but it might be a better idea for you to sit by your boy."

"My wife can do that."

"Two helping keep Joshua alive's better than only one," Fargo said. "If the going gets too rough, I'll call you to help drive the wagon."

Somewhat mollified, Cleary climbed into the rear of the wagon. Rachel hastily took his place beside Fargo and stared at him.

"You're amazing, Skye," she said softly. "I've never seen anyone who got Papa to do what he didn't want to do and with so little fuss."

"Might be I'm just getting him to do what he knows he ought to do," Fargo said, carefully turning the mule team and heading them back in the direction of Fort Davis.

"You're a better driver," Rachel said.

"You're an expert?" He grinned at her.

"Not really, but I might be a tad prejudiced in your favor," she said, grinning. Rachel moved closer, her thigh pressing warmly into his. It was as hot a day as any Fargo had encountered since reaching the desert, but somehow he did not mind.

He drove with painstaking attention paid to preventing sharp bumps and jerks so Joshua would have as smooth a trip as possible. The boy did not need added head injuries from being tossed around in the rear of the wagon.

"Why don't you stay with us when we go back toward Fort Bliss?" Rachel asked. "You are always getting us out of trouble. If you were with us all the time, you wouldn't have to ride across this terrible desert to come to our rescue."

"With your family or you?" Fargo asked, knowing what the lovely dark-haired woman really meant. At twenty-one or twenty-two, Rachel was a mite old and had to be worrying about marriage. Fargo knew she could find someone easy enough, but he doubted it was him. He looked down the dusty road and saw freedom, not a family. The feeling of being alone on the trail, roaming the high mountains and rafting down raging rivers couldn't be shared. He knew he would worry about her constantly, and that would wear on them both.

Rachel Cleary was a city girl and not meant to be on the frontier. At least, not now. She had to get used to the ways of a rougher culture. Fargo knew she would eventually.

Fargo smiled ruefully. In a year or two, Rachel would find herself a good man willing to clerk in her father's store or be a bank teller or even raise a few head of cattle. She would be some other man's wife, and content.

"I—" Rachel started to answer, then stood in the box and pointed ahead. "There, Skye, see it? Dust!"

"Riders," he agreed, his attention already fixed on the faint brown dust cloud swirling ahead. It might be a dust devil, but he doubted it. There was a lack of whirling motion to the cloud, and it moved along smoothly, following the road.

"Has a stagecoach come by since you left Fort Davis?"

"No, we haven't seen anyone but Colonel Nolan's men and you. And that horrid Apache."

A dozen small details told Fargo this was not a rumbling, lumbering Concord stage racing along the Butterfield route. Definitely riders and perhaps as many as a dozen. He touched the butt of his Colt, alarming Rachel.

"Road agents?" she asked in a small voice.

"Not too likely," he said, wondering if the Mexican bandidos might venture into this country to hold up a stagecoach or rob settlers. Alfredo and most of his gang had been arrested by the Federales, but some might have escaped.

"What are we going to do? Can we fight? Or hide? We can drive the wagon into an arroyo and hope they pass us by."

"We won't have to," Fargo said, relaxing. "That's a cavalry unit." This was the only explanation that made any sense.

Less than twenty minutes later, Fargo saw the reflection off the commanding officer's gold braid. Then the wind caught the company pennon and snapped out where he could see it.

He kept up the steady pace until he saw Colonel Nolan waving, then slowed the steadily pulling mules until they stood stock still in the center of the road.

"What are you doing returning to the fort?" Nolan asked. His eyes bored into Fargo, as if accusing him of dereliction of duty.

"Sharp Knife attacked the Clearys after you left them," Fargo said. The rest of the story spilled out in a rush as Mr. Cleary jumped down and walked around, moving gingerly to protect his own injured rib.

"So you opted to escort them back to the fort rather than capture Sharp Knife?" The sharpness in Nolan's voice put Fargo on guard. The colonel was not pleased with this decision.

"What's happened?"

"I got a heliograph message from Fort Quitman that Sharp Knife ambushed a patrol and killed three soldiers." Nolan frowned, obviously not happy at the loss of three troopers, even ones not in his command.

"One man single-handedly killed three armed soldiers?" asked Mr. Cleary, astounded. "Why, he wasn't able to kill us." Then he looked at Fargo and knew the reason they were still alive. Cleary swallowed and said, "I reckon we owe Mr. Fargo a real debt of gratitude."

"Yes," Rachel said, moving closer. Fargo saw she wanted to kiss him, but that would not have been proper in such company. Her hip rubbed against his, telling him how indebted she was to him and how she might repay some of that bill.

"Where were you heading, Colonel?" asked Fargo, uncomfortable at being the center of attention.

"Fort Quitman, to reinforce their patrols. With luck, we can capture Sharp Knife."

Fargo scratched a rough map of the territory in the dust, positioning the forts and where Sharp Knife had attacked the patrol.

"What's out here?" he asked, his finger stabbing down into a particularly dusty section of his map.

"Absolutely nothing. There's no point in going there. Sharp Knife would head north or west into Mexico."

Fargo nodded, but his mind was racing. Sharp Knife had a blood feud to settle. The one place the cavalry least expected him to go was in the middle of the desert. Fargo suspected that the Apache chief knew every watering hole and ravine in the area. Survival might be hard but not impossible for him. If he swung in a wide circle, he could swing around and approach Fort Davis from the east in a few days.

Or Fargo might intercept him on the far side of Wild Rose Pass where the Apache would least expect him.

"Can you assign a couple of soldiers to see the Clearys back to Fort Davis?" asked Fargo.

"What do you intend to do?" asked Colonel Nolan. "You can ride with us. You still work for me as a scout, and I need someone with your skill to smoke out Sharp Knife."

"You might support the troops from the other fort, but you won't find Sharp Knife there," Fargo said. "He's heading for the middle of the desert."

"Absurd," snapped Nolan. "Unless the sun has cooked his brains, not even an Apache would dare such terrain in the middle of summer." He cleared his throat, straightened his blue jacket, and glared at Fargo. "Are you coming with me?"

"No," Fargo said slowly.

"Then you'll continue escorting the civilians to the fort, where they can get medical attention. The post doctor is used to treating such head wounds."

"I'm not going to do that, either, Colonel," Fargo said. "I'm going to capture Sharp Knife."

"In the center of the driest, most dangerous stretch of West Texas?" Nolan snorted in disgust. "Sharp Knife isn't there. He wants blood. Who's there to kill? He's running, I tell you, either north to get more recruits from the Mescalero reservation in New Mexico or west to find sanctuary in Mexico."

"That might be, Colonel," Fargo said, erasing his map with the pass of his boot, "but I'm heading east."

"Then you'll do it on your own. The U.S. Army will not pay you to wander aimlessly in that godforsaken empty land."

Fargo did not explain his reasoning. Nolan did not want to hear it. Neither did Rachel nor her father. Each wanted something different from him.

All he wanted was to capture Sharp Knife.

# 17

Fargo felt Rachel's eyes on him as he rode off. It took a great deal of willpower not to look back. Colonel Nolan had given him an unpleasant send-off, but Fargo realized the cavalry commander had other missions to perform.

Fargo felt the officer was wrong in his priorities and that Sharp Knife ought to be first. The Apache renegade had killed and robbed and caused too much mayhem. With Frederickson behind bars and Alfredo Rodriguez and his gang of bandidos imprisoned on the other side of the Rio Grande, that left only Sharp Knife to contend with.

Nolan thought he was wrong, but Fargo knew deep down inside he had figured out the Indian's plan. Circle to the east where no one would be foolish enough to follow, swing south, and then west for the fort. Once there, with the troopers thinking the danger had passed, he could do all manner of mischief. Fargo thought that mischief might include killing Nolan and kidnapping Rachel again. Revenge taking that form would appeal a great deal to Sharp Knife and do much to restore him to a place of prestige among other Apaches.

"Killing me would be on his list of things to do, too," Fargo mused as he rode out into the burning desert, cut off from all civilization. He found a small patch of shade and went to ground until sundown, then started again, wondering where the watering holes were. Sharp Knife undoubtedly knew every one and used them wisely. Fargo had to rely on conserving water and strength for the fight ahead.

He rode at a steady pace, guided by the stars until he was miles into the countryside. Then he changed his route and made a sweeping curve toward the eastern mouth of Wild Rose Canyon. This led directly to Fort Davis. If Sharp Knife had followed the route Fargo thought, the Indian had to come this way.

A little after midnight, Fargo heard what sounded like a braying mule. He reined back and patted the Ovaro on the neck to keep the stallion quiet. Fargo strained to positively identify the distant sound as it floated on the imperceptible wind blowing across the still hot desert sand. It came again, but it wasn't a mule he heard. Smiling, Fargo turned his Ovaro's head toward the sound and began riding at a quicker pace.

Within twenty minutes, he topped a dune and saw the campfire burning in a hollow. Four camels were staked to one side and Corporal Williams and his three troopers crouched near the fire, drinking coffee and talking in low tones.

"Corporal!" he called to announce his presence. "It's me, Fargo."

"Mr. Fargo!" A shadowy figure jumped to his feet and waved. "Come on down and have some of this awful coffee Max boiled."

Fargo let his horse pick its way down the far side of the dune. In five minutes he had joined the soldiers, and he had a cup of terrible coffee in his hands.

"What brings you this way? I thought you were headin' north with the settlers."

Fargo knew that Williams had more than a hint of all that had passed between him and Rachel.

"The Clearys were attacked again by Sharp Knife. I had to help them, so the chief got away."

"I can't believe he's such a slippery cayuse," Williams said, shaking his head. "You grab hold of him, then you've got nothin' but thin air between your fingers."

"It seems that way at times, but I think I've outsmarted him this time." Fargo explained that he expected Sharp Knife to approach the fort through Wild Rose Pass. He did not bother saying what he thought would happen once Sharp Knife got to Fort Davis unnoticed.

"We've got the whole area under patrol, Mr. Fargo. He can't get past us," the corporal solemnly assured him. Fargo knew he would have ridden past the camel corpsmen, and they would never have been any the wiser. Sharp Knife was at home in this barren land. Even on their camels, the soldiers were no match for the Apache.

"This is a mighty big stretch of desert," Fargo reminded the corporal. "You can't patrol it all."

"Well, he might sneak by," Williams admitted. "But he wouldn't find it easy."

"No, he wouldn't," Fargo said, not wanting to argue the point. He drank some of the bitter coffee and wondered if they had eggshells to put in with the grounds. That would take away the acid cut on his tongue as the black coffee rolled over it.

"Can we help you, Mr. Fargo? It'd be a real pleasure. Colonel Nolan sends us out to get rid of us. Sometimes I think he'd rather have us all on those damned mules than embarrass him with the camels." A camel brayed loudly and spat, as if agreeing with Williams.

"You have to admit, those are mighty strange-looking critters," Fargo said.

"They can go for a month without water. And fast! On the sand they can outrun almost anything but an Arabian horse."

Fargo had heard of that breed but had never seen one. All in all, he would match his Ovaro against any fancy horse from a desert country on the other side of the world.

"You might be of some help," Fargo said. "I don't have eyes in the back of my head, and there's a powerful lot of desert to cover. It's nothing more than a guess, but I figure Sharp Knife ought to reach the pass sometime after sunrise. You willing to help?"

"Why, nothin' would pleasure us more, right, boys?" The corporal glared at the three soldiers with him until they reluctantly joined in. Fargo was not sure how he would use them, but in one respect Corporal Williams was right. The more men hunting for Sharp Knife, the better chance they had of finding the elusive Mescalero.

"You think that's the varmint, Mr. Fargo?" asked the corporal. Fargo had climbed to the top of a rocky ridge to study the roads funneling into Wild Rose Pass. To the north billowed a small dust cloud. Possibly a single rider or maybe a dust devil. As he watched, Fargo decided it was a rider coming from the direction Sharp Knife was most likely to use.

"I wish we had a pair of field glasses," Fargo said, shielding his eyes with the brim of his hat and trying to make sense of the situation. The corporal had given his to the post quartermaster in exchange for a few pounds of the terrible coffee. If they rode out to cut off the rider's escape without knowing who they were approaching, all of them had to commit to the trap. That was all right if this was really Sharp Knife. If the Apache war chief sent another brave ahead as a cat's-paw, he would escape easily. If this was just another rider, having no connection with Sharp Knife or Frederickson or the Mexico banditos, the camel-riding troopers would spook him something fierce.

And Sharp Knife might get away if he was watching.

"Let's go after him," Fargo said, swiftly coming to a decision. This was a desolate land. Travelers were less likely to come from the north, as this rider was doing, than from the east or the south and San Antonio. The camels grunted and squawked and got their ungainly bodies moving. Fargo had to smile at the unearthly sight of the knobby-kneed "ships of the desert" starting to trot. Then he found himself hard pressed to keep up with them. Their dinner plate–sized feet refused to sink into the soft sand, and the camels' long legs ate up the distance quickly. The only place Fargo's Ovaro had the advantage was on rockier land where the camels picked their way almost gingerly to protect those huge feet.

"He's runnin', Mr. Fargo. He spotted us and is high-tailin' it!"

"Spread out and go after him," Fargo said. They still had not positively identified the rider as the Mescalero, but taking off like this meant the rider had something to hide.

Fargo followed a rocky draw, dodged spiny branches of ocotillo, and then got his horse up a stony embankment where he could see what was going on. He smiled from ear to ear.

"Sharp Knife!" he cried. The Apache jerked around and glared at him. Sharp Knife made an obscene gesture, yelled something in Apache that Fargo did not understand, and then the chase was on. Sharp Knife put his heels to his pony's flanks and shot off like a rocket.

The camels closed the distance fast, with Fargo trailing over the sandy stretch. Then Sharp Knife realized his horse's disadvantage in the shifting sands and turned back toward the foothills and rockier ground. The camel soldiers fell back, but Fargo began gaining on the renegade. Before long, he found himself alone on Sharp Knife's trail, Corporal Williams and his soldiers having to pick their way through the sharp-rock fields.

Fargo knew Sharp Knife was clever and began looking for possible traps. Because of this wariness, he slowed. Now and then Fargo stopped entirely and turned slowly, listening hard for the sound of the Apache's horse. All he heard were the normal desert sounds mingling with those from the mountain pass. Wind whining, a distant coyote, even the ghastly sounds made by the camels struggling to keep up far behind.

He heard nothing of Sharp Knife. Fargo drew his Henry and laid it across the saddle in front of him. The feeling of being watched grew, but Fargo had to keep going. He was so close. He felt it deep in his gut, but where had Sharp Knife gone?

Dismounting, Fargo began examining the stony ground. Sharp Knife was riding an unshod horse, which worked against Fargo now. No sharp, shiny cuts on rocks from horseshoes. No click-click of metal against stone.

"Where did you go?" he muttered, kneeling to study the ground intently. Sharp Knife might have turned into a ghost and simply fluttered off for all the tracks he left behind. Fargo got down on his belly and carefully looked over the terrain and found nothing.

Disgusted at his bad luck, he stood and brushed himself off before Williams and the other camel troopers arrived.

"Where'd the son of a bitch go, Mr. Fargo?"

"I don't know. Not far, unless I miss my guess," Fargo said, thinking hard. This was wild, almost unexplored land for all the travelers on their way to Fort Davis that passed through the area. Sharp Knife knew the land like the back of his hand, and he had found a hidey-hole.

"You reckon he was going to attack the fort?"

"Maybe not," Fargo said, an idea coming to him. It was dangerous and not one Colonel Nolan would go along with, but Fargo saw no other way of flushing out Sharp Knife. "He headed here for a reason."

"Might be that he has a rendezvous point there," Williams said.

"That's my thought exactly," Fargo said, "and I know how to find it without turning over every last rock in the desert."

He mounted and headed through the pass for Fort Davis. As much as he hated letting Sharp Knife go now, it was only for a short time. The Apache chief had the upper hand, but Fargo held the trump card. And it was time to play it.

# 18

Fargo felt like a thief in the night sneaking into Fort Davis, but he didn't want anyone to see him. Especially Colonel Nolan. All the way to the fort from Wild Rose Pass, Fargo had considered asking the colonel to go along with his harebrained scheme, and not once did he imagine the officer agreeing.

A quarter mile from the fort, Fargo tethered his Ovaro and went the rest of the way on foot. The fort was alive with dancing late-afternoon shadows, letting him get into the grounds without being spotted by the guard. The heat from another scorching day had taken its toll on the sentry, making him sluggish and not a little bit sleepy. If Fargo had been Sharp Knife, the guard would have died with a slit throat. As it was, Fargo only wanted to reach the guardhouse.

He hesitated when he got near the stockade where Big Red Frederickson was being held. Two guards outside were both dozing in the shade on the north side. This was the perfect time to put his scheme into effect, but Fargo held back. He had neglected one small detail in his planning.

If he let Frederickson out, the gunrunner would get a horse and have a fifteen-minute—or longer—head start because Fargo had to run back to where he had left his horse, then pick up Frederickson's trail. Worse, the gunrunner might be clumsy in his escape and alert the guards, making Fargo's role in how he got away obvious. A turn of luck would see *him* in the stockade and the gunrunner riding away scot-free.

Fargo needed help, but he couldn't ask just anyone.

Corporal Williams remained on patrol on the far side of the pass, hunting for Sharp Knife's hiding place. Fargo doubted the young soldier would find it. The Apache chief was too wily for that. The only way of flushing out his quarry was to follow Frederickson. Sharp Knife had come this way for a reason, and Fargo thought that might be freeing the gunrunner. If Frederickson didn't make a beeline for Sharp Knife's hideout, Fargo knew he could snare him quickly and return him to the colonel's custody. There would be questions asked and answers that would be painful to give, but Fargo could always point out that no harm had been done.

If his plan worked, he would bag both Sharp Knife and Frederickson again.

Fargo crept along, using the lengthening shadows and knowing he had to wait until nightfall. The best time to spring Frederickson would probably be when the soldiers were called to mess. Fargo figured he'd have to wait about an hour.

He needed an ally. A smile slowly crossed his face as he headed for the barracks. A quick search showed that the Cleary family had not been housed here. He turned to the hospital and soon found the room where Joshua lay. The boy seemed alert and talkative, but Rachel did her best to keep him quiet. The rest of the family had been billeted in the hallway outside, owing to lack of bunk space for them. Fargo guessed this was also Nolan's way of getting them to move along faster. He didn't cotton much to civilians eating his soldiers' food and sleeping in their beds.

Fargo rapped lightly against the window frame to get Rachel's attention. She looked up. Her eyes went wide when she saw him. The dark-haired woman started to call out to him, but he put his finger to his lips, cautioning her to silence. Then he motioned that he wanted to talk to her outside. She nodded, got Joshua settled down again and then hastily left.

He went to the north side of the hospital and waited for her to come out.

"Skye! I didn't know if I'd see you again." She threw her arms around his neck and kissed him squarely on the lips. He felt the pressure of her firm young breasts crushing into his chest and smelled the clean scent of her long dark hair. Rachel didn't put up any fuss.

"I need your help," he said.

"Anything! I—"

"This will be dangerous, and if you're caught, you could get into big trouble."

Rachel giggled like a schoolgirl. "You want to, well, you know? I wouldn't mind being caught with you a million times over!"

Fargo had to grin. Her desires were transparent—and matched his own.

"Not that," he said.

"Oh," Rachel said, heaving a mock sigh of resignation. "See how you are? Use me, then discard me." Her words said one thing, but her body told him a different story. She pulled him closer so her nimble fingers could begin working at his gun belt and the buttons holding up his trousers.

"I need to ask you if—" was the furthest he got before she kissed him hard on the lips. Then she released him and stared into his blue eyes.

"I'll do anything you want, Skye, no matter how dangerous."

"You don't know what I want you to do," he said lamely.

"I think I do," she said, her fingers fishing around in the front of his pants until she found a steadily growing organ and took it firmly in hand. She ran her fingers up and down it a few times until it had become long and hard and almost painful to him.

Fargo wanted to ask her to help him free Frederickson, but the words stuck in his throat. It was too much to ask of her. He had no right. He shouldn't.

Then Fargo kissed her lips and eyes and throat. Rachel moaned softly and melted like butter in his arms. They sank down so Fargo was sitting on the hospital steps and Rachel was straddling his waist. She twisted and turned and got her skirts hiked up.

He couldn't see what was going on. He didn't have to. He felt it. Her fleecy triangle brushed across the tip of his manhood as she positioned herself. Then the lovely woman's hips lowered. He felt the head of his throbbing shaft touch the softness of her nether lips. When Rachel simply relaxed, her body dropped, now supported on his splayed knees. This drove him all the way up into her tight, wet female passage.

Fargo grunted at the sudden entry. Rachel's reaction was even more intense. She shuddered and buried her face in his shoulder. For a moment they sat there. Then she began moving her hips in small, slow circles that stirred him around in her until jolts of carnal electricity turned into lightning bolts.

He held her close, kissing her throat and nibbling her earlobes. Then she bent backward, driving her hips down harder into his lap. This caused his manhood to sink even deeper into her. She arched her back, popping the buttons on her blouse. Fargo bent forward so he could lick her breasts and the lust-hardened nipples at the crests. He whirled his tongue around, licking and then sucking as she kept up the motion with her hips.

Together they pushed each other's passions to the breaking point. When Fargo bit gently on one cherry-red bud, Rachel exploded in ecstasy. Her unrestrained excitement lasted forever, or so it seemed to Fargo. Her clutching tunnel squeezed down powerfully on him, as if she were trying to milk him.

"Yes, oh, I'm on fire inside, Skye, so good, so, oohhh!"

The deep shudders hit her again. This time her hips went wild. She bobbed up and down, lifting fast and driving down with all the power and lust locked within her trim young body. She ground her crotch into his.

When he felt her explode lustfully a third time, Fargo was no longer able to hold back himself. His arms circled her waist and held her down as he lifted off the wooden step and tried to impale her fully with his fleshy spike. He rotated his hips and held back his own tumultuous release as long as he could. Then desire outraced even iron control.

He erupted like a volcano. This caused the woman to thrash about, moaning and sobbing and clawing his back, trying to get even more enjoyment out of their coupling. All too soon for both of them, the passions faded and left them clinging weakly to each other.

"Oh, Skye, I'm going to miss this. Why don't you come with us?"

"I can't," he said, not wanting to admit this might be the last time he and Rachel would be together like this.

"Let me stay with you, then. Papa doesn't need me. He has Joshua and Abel. We can—" Rachel broke off and took a deep breath, as if facing reality. "I know there's no place for me riding alongside you. But maybe—"

Fargo held her and that satisfied Rachel for a spell. Then she got her legs under her and stood, skirts dropping around her sleek, slender legs. She stared at his groin and grinned.

"My, my, what *have* you been doing?" she said jokingly.

"I've been up to no good," Fargo said, buttoning himself up.

"You've been up," Rachel said, "but I wouldn't call it no good. I'd call it mighty fine." Her cheerfulness evaporated and then she asked, "What do you want me to do?"

"This is dangerous and you—"

"Skye, I don't care. If you want me to help, I will. Any way I can."

He told her exactly how to let Frederickson out of the stockade without the gunrunner knowing who did it. What he could not tell Rachel was how to avoid being caught by the soldiers and locked up herself for letting such a dangerous man out of jail.

Fargo shivered in the cold dawn. The longer he sat and waited for Frederickson to show up, the more doubt ate away at his guts. Sharp Knife had come back for some reason. For a rendezvous with Frederickson? Or to get revenge against the cavalry? Or some other reason Fargo had no inkling about? He had to believe Frederickson would hightail it from the Fort Davis stockade and go straight to where Sharp Knife had gone to

**148**

ground if they had an agreed upon rendezvous nearby. It would be private, out of sight and, for them, safe.

The Apache needed rifles and men to fire them, and Frederickson was most likely to supply part of that deadly equation because he needed the money.

If Frederickson even knew the Apache chief was in the area. Fargo heaved a sigh. There was a great deal of risk in the plan he had so impetuously implicated Rachel in. He believed in his own skills to recapture Frederickson easily, but the rest of it, the part about the gunrunner going to the spot where Sharp Knife was hiding, worried him more and more.

Fargo perked up when he heard the quick clicking of horse hooves sailing on the faint morning breeze. He shivered, took a deep breath, and caught scent of a man and horse, then got ready. One horse, one rider—who else but Frederickson coming from his easy escape from Fort Davis?

At least, Fargo hoped this was true.

Big Red Frederickson passed within fifty yards of where Fargo waited. He never saw the Trailsman because he was so intent on getting away from Fort Davis. Fargo was worried that Colonel Nolan would find that his prisoner had flown the coop and would send out a company of troopers to recapture him. That would make the gunrunner take off for Mexico.

A smile crossed Fargo's lips. If Frederickson had worried about that, he would have headed west, not east, from the fort. He was heading somewhere other than across the Rio Grande. His heels tapped the Ovaro's sides, and Fargo eased the horse onto the trail when Frederickson rode out of sight. Tracking him was easy, but avoiding the sharp-eyed Apache chief's notice was something else.

Fargo was worried about springing a trap, and something else began inching into his mind. It itched and irritated and finally built to the point that he could identify the problem.

Someone was tracking *him*.

Fargo realized the danger surrounding him. Frederickson was ahead. The only one who could possibly be behind him on the trail was Sharp Knife. Which would he capture? Let the gunrunner escape and capture Sharp Knife? Or catch up with Frederickson, take him, and fight it out with the Apache? Neither struck him as a good choice because of the danger one—or both—would get away from him.

Without consciously coming to a conclusion, Fargo veered sharply off the trail, drew his Henry, and then found a spot where he could cover the trail. He doubted Sharp Knife would give up just because Fargo had the drop on him, but the Trailsman had to try. If the Apache chief wanted a fight, he would get it in spades.

The Ovaro trotted off and found a dry patch of grass to nibble. Fargo levered a round into the Henry's chamber, lifted it to his shoulder, and waited. The sound of an approaching horse put Fargo on edge. He sighted down the barrel and got the bright bead resting properly in the front notch sight. His finger tensed on the trigger as the rider came around a bend in the trail.

Fargo's eyes went wide and he lowered the rifle.

"Rachel!" he called. "What are you doing here?"

Fargo was not sure he wanted to hear the answer.

# 19

"Skye, you scared me," the woman said. She rode over to him, staring at the way he held the rifle. Her eyes went wide as she realized how close she had come to being shot. "You . . . you would have fired at me!"

"Why are you here? Did the colonel catch you letting Frederickson out?" That was the only reason he could think she had taken the horse and ridden into the cold desert. She, of all people, had to know the dangers lurking in the West Texas countryside.

"Oh, no, nothing like that," she said, laughing. "I avoided the guards. They were asleep so no one saw me. That horrible gunrunner got away, as you said he would, when I opened the lock on his cell door, but it occurred to me that you might need help tracking him."

Fargo stared at her, speechless. If she had lassoed Frederickson and rode ten feet behind him, Rachel could never have kept up with him the way Fargo could.

"He came this way. I thought you'd like to know that."

"I saw him." Fargo struggled to understand what was going through her pretty head. She had helped him by releasing Frederickson, but what on earth had possessed her to follow the gunrunner?

"Oh, good, then you don't need me," she said, tears welling in her blue eyes. "I am just trying to help."

Fargo held his tongue. The only thing she was doing was putting her own life at risk—and almost guaranteeing Frederickson's escape. Fargo could not look after Rachel and hunt down the rendezvous point at the same time.

"You have to go back," he said. "It's too dangerous for you out here."

"Let me come along. I've done well so far, haven't I?" she said.

"Yes, but—" Fargo cut off his answer, tipped his head to one side, and listened hard. Horses. At least a dozen. The thunder of their hooves died quickly, meaning they were not more than a half mile off.

"What is it?"

"Hush," Fargo said, turning from her and sniffing hard at the nighttime air. He caught the faintest whiff of burning mesquite wood. And with it came the odor of coffee.

"Skye, really."

He wanted to send her back to Fort Davis, where it was safe, but getting there now was more dangerous than he could reckon. Sharp Knife's rendezvous with Frederickson was proceeding faster than he had anticipated. Without any firm knowledge, Fargo had thought Sharp Knife had a watering hole somewhere in the middle of Wild Rose Pass rather than on the Fort Davis side. Fargo realized how dangerous it was to make such suppositions. He would have ridden up to Sharp Knife and probably gotten himself ambushed.

"Is Frederickson meeting the Apaches?" she asked.

"That's the way I read it," Fargo said. His thoughts were jumbled as he wondered if she could return to Fort Davis without being heard or if she should go to earth here and not move. Somehow, he doubted Rachel was capable of that when so much was at stake.

"Come with me, but don't make a sound," he said. Rachel smiled brightly, then the smile died when she saw how serious Fargo was.

"This is bad, isn't it?"

"It's not just Frederickson and Sharp Knife," he told her. "That would be hard enough, but there are more with them. Probably renegade Apaches off the reservation feeling their oats."

Rachel swallowed hard, realizing the predicament she had ridden into. Without saying a word more, Fargo set off on foot in the direction of the camp. Before he had gone more than fifty paces, he motioned Rachel to a halt and then pulled her to the ground.

"Sharp Knife's got braves out patrolling," he said. Rachel did not see the Apache guard, even when Fargo pointed him out to her. He had been right not letting her go off on her own, but keeping her with him increased the danger to them both and made it more difficult to capture either Sharp Knife or Frederickson.

Fargo lay belly down on the ground for almost ten minutes, determining that only one Apache stood guard. He heaved a deep sigh, then moved forward, a shadow among shadows. As he approached the Apache, he tossed a pebble to the side. Distracted, the Apache jumped to his feet and fully exposed himself.

Fargo moved like a striking snake. His left arm circled the brave's throat and clamped down on the man's windpipe while his right jerked the rifle from an increasingly feeble grip. Fargo followed the man to the ground and made sure he was unconscious.

"Skye, what are you going to do?" came Rachel's whisper.

"The trail back to the fort is open," he said, not knowing for sure if it was. "This was the only guard Sharp Knife had posted. Go fetch Colonel Nolan and have him come with every last trooper he can round up."

"What'll I tell him? That I let Frederickson out and—"

"Tell him whatever you have to," Fargo said, unwilling to argue with her over it. "Just get him here!"

"Oh, Skye, I'm so sorry. I fouled up everything. I—"

Fargo grabbed her, pulled her to him, and kissed her hard to silence her. Rachel gasped and stepped away, her fingertips lightly touching her mouth.

"Go on, get moving," he ordered.

Rachel backtracked to where they had left their horses. He cringed when he heard the pounding noise of her too-rapid retreat. Rachel galloped off, throwing caution to the wind. He hoped there weren't other guards in this direction. They would hear and wonder who was in such a powerful hurry this late at night. Fargo listened and waited but heard nothing to tell him

Rachel's precipitous retreat had been noticed. He stripped the knocked-out brave of his weapons, then tied him up and gagged him using rawhide strips cut from the man's own buckskin shirt.

Only then did Fargo go after Frederickson and Sharp Knife. He got within twenty feet of the campfire Sharp Knife had built. The men sat close to the fire to ward off the chilly night air and spoke in low, guarded tones. Fargo counted the Apaches drifting around the campfire. At least six and no more than ten. Even ignoring the one he had left tied up behind him, Fargo knew he was in no position to attack. All he could do was sit and wait for Rachel to bring the colonel and his soldiers.

Fargo fumed at how he had miscalculated. If only Sharp Knife and Frederickson had been here, he could have taken them both. He had not thought Sharp Knife would have recruited so many braves this fast. Or maybe he had been wrong and this was a recognized rendezvous point for all the Apaches. It was almost on the doorstep of Fort Davis and ought to have been found a long time ago by Nolan's patrols.

He settled down, rifle across his knees, and watched. "Ought to have been" and "should have been" meant nothing. From the way Frederickson and Sharp Knife talked and drank the coffee boiling on the fire, they were settled in for the night. That gave Rachel plenty of time to fetch Nolan.

Fargo still worried as he sat silently, watching and waiting.

He began to grow increasingly uneasy after fifteen minutes when Sharp Knife and Frederickson stopped their close talk and moved apart. The gunrunner seemed in a fine mood, laughing and joking with the Apache braves circling the camp like restlessly circling vultures waiting for something to die. Sharp Knife was less jovial, sitting with his arms crossed and staring into the fire.

The Apache chief suddenly shot to his feet and called to Frederickson, "I will give you the money. We need guns."

"And you shall have them. Help me with my little

problem, and I'll see you and your braves get all the rifles you can carry."

"I will smuggle you across the river," Sharp Knife said. "And I will give you the gold. How do you intend to steal so many rifles?"

"I already have them, my good man," Frederickson said. "I cached them not far from here. You can have them within the hour, if you have the money."

"We could torture the hiding place from you," suggested Sharp Knife.

"Surely, you could," Frederickson said amiably. "But you'll be needing more. Don't think a dozen rifles will go far when you have hundreds of warriors riding behind you. I can get more. I know how. I have connections in Mexico. Keep the cavalry off my neck, get me across the Rio Grande, and I'll see that you have all the rifles and ammo you can carry."

"Done," Sharp Knife said. "Let us go now."

"The gold, Sharp Knife, the gold. I'll need it when I reach Mexico."

"Like you, I have hidden treasures. Give me the guns, then you get the gold and your safe passage. Do not trust me, and the cavalry colonel will hang you."

"I reckon you might be right about that," said the gunrunner. "We've done business for a year now, and you've always been a straight shooter. Let's ride."

Fargo lifted his rifle and instinctively followed Frederickson with it. Then he lowered it, seeing Sharp Knife and the rest of the Apaches were going with him. Fargo wondered how far Rachel had gotten on her return to the fort and if he could expect help soon—or at all.

If he let Frederickson give the rifles to Sharp Knife, there would be no stopping the Apaches. The fight had to be here and it had to be now. Even if he attacked single-handedly.

As the gunrunner started to mount his horse, Fargo acted. He fired his rifle through the tight knot of horses, spooking them. Frederickson was thrown to the ground. Sharp Knife had not even reached his pony, which bolted at the near passage of a piece of whining lead.

Fargo fired again, scattering the horses and making it difficult for the Apaches to fight.

The confusion lasted only a few seconds. Sharp Knife was a good leader and got his braves to cover. Fargo sporadically fired, not wanting to give away his position but needing to keep them pinned down.

For how long?

He had no idea.

"Soldiers!" shouted Frederickson. "They followed me!"

"No," Sharp Knife said. "There is only one." The chief waved, and a brave to his left started circling. Then one on his right flank duplicated the maneuver. They would come up behind Fargo in a few minutes if he stayed put. And if he retreated, he would lose both the gunrunner and the renegade chief.

Fargo began firing methodically, aiming for exposed arms and legs and heads. He winged a couple Apaches, causing some consternation among them, but he only revealed his own position. Both Sharp Knife and Frederickson saw this immediately.

"There he is," shouted Frederickson. "Let's go get the varmint."

Fargo heard the two braves coming up behind him and saw a half dozen dark shapes approaching him from the front. He knew which two were Sharp Knife and Frederickson and tried to put bullets into them. The hail of slugs coming his way made accurate shooting impossible. He dropped to his belly and began slithering to his right, hoping to avoid being seen.

One brave coming up behind him spotted the move and directed the rest after him. Fargo got his feet under him and, keeping low, ran as hard as he could. He fired until his Henry's magazine emptied, and then he used his six-shooter to keep the pursuers at bay.

He got into rocks above the campsite. In the guttering fire he saw the watering hole and the pool partly hidden by large boulders. Access to this spot was limited, making it perfect to defend. Then he stopped worrying about attacking and started worrying about staying alive. Three braves came up the narrow path through the towering rocks after him.

Unable to take time to reload fully, Fargo got off three quick shots. The first struck the leading warrior, dropping him to his knees. The two following him stopped and did what they could for their wounded comrade. This gave Fargo the chance to reload his Henry.

"Fifteen rounds," he muttered to himself. This was all the ammo he had left. Even the best shot in the world wasn't going to take out one man with every shot.

Fargo put up a good fight, but the tide of battle went against him when the Apaches gained the high ground behind him. He shot one who foolishly silhouetted himself against the night sky and knew at least two others were there and coming down after him. He couldn't fire uphill and back down the path at the same time.

He couldn't stand and fight. He couldn't run. Retreat was cut off. All Fargo could do was die.

If this was the end of the trail, he wanted as many of the Apaches as possible to ride the Ghost Pony with him.

"There!" shouted Sharp Knife, rising from the rocks below. "There he is!"

Fargo started to poke his head up like a prairie dog leaving its burrow to take the shot at the Apache chief, then hesitated. Sharp Knife was no fool. He had to know he exposed himself to fire. That meant . . .

Fargo threw himself to the side, barely avoiding a bullet from behind. Sharp Knife had tried to decoy him into revealing himself. Fargo fired blindly uphill, hoping to drive the unseen sniper back. Four shots. Five. Six. Then he stopped firing. He wasn't sure if he had more than two or three rounds left in his rifle.

His Colt was empty and his rifle nearly so. He had to make the final rounds count.

Fargo looked for a better shot, then ducked down. The number of bullets flying through the air would have turned him into a ragged, bloody corpse. It took him a few seconds to puzzle out what bothered him about the furious attack. Then it came to him. The bullets were not ricocheting off rocks around him, yet the Apaches knew where he was.

Poking his head up for a quick peek, Fargo wanted to let out a cry of joy. Rachel had fetched Colonel Nolan's troopers!

Fargo heard sounds behind him and rolled over, bringing up his rifle. He pulled the trigger when he saw the Apache above him. The hammer fell on an empty chamber. He had miscounted the rounds he had left. Then he was fighting for his life, the Apache driving a knife straight for his face.

As quickly as the attack started, it ended. The Apache went limp and sagged on him. Fargo pushed the Indian away and looked up into Colonel Nolan's clouded face.

"You do things in the damnedest ways, Fargo. I wish you'd let me know what was going on."

"Frederickson," he said quickly, getting to his feet. "He's—"

"In custody."

"What about Sharp Knife?"

"Didn't see him, but—" Colonel Nolan spoke to empty air. Fargo was glad the gunrunner had been recaptured, but he had to make a clean sweep and bring down Sharp Knife, too. That had been the reason for all his finagling and planning.

As he went, he scooped up fallen rifles and got usable ammo for both his Colt and his Henry.

"Skye, you're safe! I didn't have to go all the way to the fort. The colonel was already on the trail, and coming after me!" babbled Rachel.

Fargo had suspected as much. The distance was too great to expect the cavalry to arrive when it did if Rachel had to rouse the colonel, get his men mustered and on the trail, and then find Sharp Knife's campground in the dark.

"You pulled my fat out of the fire," he told her.

"I'd rather pull something else," she said.

"Not now. Sharp Knife's hightailed it. I want him bad." Fargo left the dark-haired woman pleading with him to let the cavalry hunt down the Apache chief, but he knew it would never happen. Sharp Knife was too cunning. He had used a hideout right under the cavalry's nose. Where else might he find refuge?

Fargo had to track him down.

He grabbed a spare Indian pony, rode it back to where his Ovaro stood impatiently, as if the horse wanted to get to the pursuit as much as Fargo. He knew better than to gallop for long, but Fargo did anyway. Catching Sharp Knife was more important than pacing the horse now. Catch the Apache chief quickly and the horse could eat oats and rest for a week.

Fargo raced into the night, glancing down at the ground occasionally to be sure he was on the right track. Sharp Knife had had no time to hide his trail. The Mescalero did not even try, making it easier for Fargo to catch up. When he topped a sandy ridge and looked down into the harsh nighttime desert, a slow smile crossed his lips. Corporal Williams and his patrol had effectively cut off Sharp Knife's retreat, forcing the Apache back in Fargo's direction.

The camels spooked Sharp Knife's horse, making it rear and buck. By the time he had doubled back, Fargo was ready for him. A clump of mesquite provided Fargo adequate cover. He rested his Ovaro, waiting, waiting, waiting.

The pounding hooves told him the moment of truth was at hand. As Sharp Knife trotted past, Fargo struck. He galloped out at an angle, taking Sharp Knife by surprise. Using his rifle as a club, he swung. Sharp Knife was quick enough to avoid catching the metal barrel on the side of his head, but was not fast enough to avoid Fargo's second attack.

The Trailsman awkwardly launched himself from his saddle, arms reaching out. His rifle hit Sharp Knife's arm, and then Fargo's shoulder crashed into the Indian's ribs. Sharp Knife fell from the saddle and crashed to the ground, momentarily stunned. By the time he had his wits about him, he looked up and saw Fargo sighting down the barrel of his Colt.

"Don't try it," Fargo said.

"You will kill me now," Sharp Knife said, taking a deep breath of resignation.

"No," Fargo said, "I'm going to let Corporal Williams arrest you."

Fargo wasn't sure who was the most surprised, Sharp Knife or the corporal, who had come trotting up on his foul-smelling, bad-tempered camel.

"That's a mighty generous reward, Colonel," Fargo said, staring at the paper Nolan had given him.

"All you have to do to collect it is present it to the paymaster down in San Antonio."

Fargo nodded. This was Nolan's way of getting rid of him once and for all. Nothing had been said about Frederickson's escape because the gunrunner was safely locked up alongside Sharp Knife. Fargo guessed he might be in that same stockade if either of them had escaped.

But they had not.

"Are you transferring your prisoners to San Antonio?" Fargo asked.

"We've got quite a party heading in that direction," Nolan said with satisfaction. "I don't see any reason not to send them along—with you and fifty of my men."

"And me and my family, Colonel," spoke up Mr. Cleary.

"You have finally decided San Antonio is a better place to set up a store than Fort Bliss?" the colonel asked.

Fargo's eyes widened at this. Then he smiled.

Rachel returned the smile. They would be riding the trail together as far as San Antonio. Turning the prisoners over to the district military commander meant the end of both Sharp Knife's and Frederickson's reign of terror.

And he would be accompanying Rachel and her family.

It could get better, but Fargo couldn't decide how.

"When do we leave?"

"Anxious to get on the trail?" asked Colonel Nolan.

"You might say that," Fargo said, looking past the colonel. Rachel had already climbed into her family's battered wagon. "In fact, you *can* say that."

## LOOKING FORWARD!
### The following is the opening section from the next novel in the exciting *Trailsman* series from Signet:

## THE TRAILSMAN #235

## FLATHEAD FURY

*1861—In the wilds of Montana, one man's lust for power threatened to unleash a bloodbath that would stain the wilderness scarlet. . . .*

The big man in buckskins squinted up from under his hat brim at the bright afternoon sun. He had been in the saddle since before daybreak and looked forward to stopping for the night, but it would be another five to six hours yet.

Skye Fargo spied a golden eagle soaring high on air currents in search of prey, its wings outspread. Off among a cluster of spruce trees a jay squawked noisily and was answered by one of its kind. Much closer, almost from under the hooves of his pinto stallion, rose a rapid chittering. Fargo's lake-blue eyes lowered to a feisty chipmunk that was scolding him for daring to intrude on its domain. Dwarfed by the Ovaro, the tiny curmudgeon threw a fit, prancing and chattering in a frenzy.

Fargo smiled. He loved the wilderness. To him it was home. He knew the creatures that lived there as well as city dwellers knew their neighbors. He knew the habits of every animal, knew the sounds they made and the tracks they left. So when a faint whine fell on his ears his interest perked and he tilted his head to pinpoint the direction it came from.

It was a low, pitiable whine, such as a wolf or coyote might make. Wolves, though, were seldom abroad at that time of the day and coyotes ordinarily preferred open country to dense woodland.

Fargo veered aside to investigate. Instinctively he lowered his right hand to the smooth butt of the Colt on his hip. He doubted whatever was out there posed a threat, but it didn't pay to be careless.

The whining grew louder. The Ovaro pricked its ears but otherwise showed no alarm.

Fargo threaded through some ponderosa pines and came to a thicket. He reined wide to go around when suddenly some of the thin branches shook. Halting, he peered into the thicket's depths, not quite knowing what to expect but certainly not expecting to find what he did.

A small, scruffy mongrel was on its belly, its long hair matted and dirty, its wide eyes brimming with fear. It had an oval face, a button nose, and floppy ears. Around its neck was a leather collar to which a rope leash had been attached, and the leash was tangled fast.

"Where did you come from?" Fargo wondered aloud. To his knowledge there wasn't a town or settlement within a hundred miles. Nor had he seen any sign of an Indian village. Dismounting, he sank onto his hands and knees.

The dog whined louder and tried to back away, but it couldn't go anywhere thanks to the tangled leash.

"I won't hurt you, little one," Fargo said. Removing his hat, he turned on his side, squeezed into the thicket, and crawled forward. The mongrel trembled and whimpered as if afraid he were going to eat it. "Give me a minute and I'll have you out of here."

Easier said than done, Fargo discovered. The thicket was so dense, the branches so intertwined, he had to bend or break them to force his way deeper. Sharp tips pricked his forehead and cheeks. One nearly nicked an eye. The closer he came, the more the dog quaked, and when he was almost within reach it covered its eyes with its front paws and howled in terror.

Fargo couldn't help laughing. "You're about as brave as they come," he joked, extending his right arm as far as he was able. He couldn't quite reach. Wriggling another few inches, he patted the mongrel's head to soothe it and the dog stopped howling. Before he could rescue it he had to unravel the leash, which took some doing. The thing was virtually in a knot. He pried and tugged for minutes before he loosened the rope enough to make headway.

The dog had lowered its paws and was watching with intent interest. It had stopped trembling but still whined pitiably every now and then.

"Almost there," Fargo said, unwinding a last loop from around a last stem. A strong jerk, and it slid free. Gripping the dog's collar, Fargo carefully pulled the animal toward him. The dog offered no resistance, not even when he slipped his other hand underneath and drew it to his chest.

"Rest a while," he said, rubbing the dog behind its ears. "You're safe now." Hardly were the words out of his mouth than the dog slumped in exhaustion and drifted into deep slumber.

Fargo separated the leash from the collar. Whoever tied it had used four large, rather crude knots. As the last came undone he noticed a pair of initials someone had stitched in the leather: JJ. Did they stand for the dog's name, he wondered, or for the owner's?

The sun dipped lower in the western sky. Fargo saw no evidence of a homestead or a ranch, no sign of anything that would explain the dog's presence in the middle of nowhere. He was beginning to think that maybe the mongrel had wandered from a passing wagon train even though he wasn't anywhere near any of the trails they regularly used. Then he emerged from the forest into a broad clearing on the crest of a sawtooth ridge and spotted a cluster of buildings in a lush valley below.

Fargo had heard nothing about there being a settlement in that area. Many miles to the east there were a few, and to the south a couple had recently sprouted, but the country in the vicinity of the southern end of Flathead Lake was supposed to be virgin territory, unspoiled by human hands. It was why he was there. He wanted some time to himself, wanted to camp out by the lake for a week or two and not see another human soul.

Drawing rein, Fargo studied the buildings. He counted over two dozen arrayed along a single dusty street. Scores of cattle grazed the surrounding grassland. The sight was depressing. Each year more and more pilgrims flocked west; each year more and more of the frontier was eaten away.

"We might as well see if anyone owns you," Fargo said to the sleeping dog, and lightly touched his spurs to the Ovaro.

Deadfalls delayed their descent. It was a full forty-five minutes before Fargo neared the bottom of the slope and heard the distinctive thud of an ax striking wood. He reined toward the source.

A man in a straw hat and a boy of eight or nine, both dressed in store-bought clothes, were near the tree line. The boy was watching the man chop down a sapling. Father and son, Fargo reckoned, moving closer. Beyond the tree line a wagon had been parked, and a similarly dressed stocky townsman was stacking downed saplings in the wagon bed.

Neither the father nor his son noticed the Ovaro until it was almost on top of them. "You're lucky I'm not a hostile," Fargo said, bringing the stallion to a stop.

Both spun in alarm. The man hiked the ax to protect

himself while the boy bounded behind him and peeked out.

"I don't mean you any harm," Fargo assured them. "I'm on my way to the settlement yonder. Does it have a name?"

"That it does, mister," the man found his voice. He had a haggard look about him, as if he hadn't slept well in a while. "It's called Wolfrik." He spelled the name. "Named after the man who founded it."

"The duke," the boy chimed in. A freckle-faced stringbean, he smiled shyly and admired the pinto.

"Duke?" Fargo repeated.

The man nodded. "Duke Otto Wolfrik. He moved here from a small country called Transia about two years ago." His tone implied he wasn't very fond of Wolfrik's founder.

"He lives in a great big house," the boy added, pointing to the north. "Biggest house I ever did see. It has more rooms than all the homes in Wolfrik put together."

"Is that a fact?" Fargo said. It didn't surprise him. In recent years wealthy Europeans had shown a keen interest in the untamed lands west of the Mississippi. Many had hired noted scouts to guide them on tours of the prairie and the Rockies. Some liked it so much they decided to stay and invested heavily in land.

The man lowered the ax. He had a frank, honest air about him, typical of hardworking settlers everywhere. "Where's my manners? I'm Frank Seaver. I run the general store. This here is my son, Johnny. We're cutting down trees to build a corral."

"The duke let us!" Johnny said cheerfully.

"Let you?" Fargo didn't see where Otto Wolfrik had any say in the matter. It was a free country, as the saying went, and a man could build himself a corral whenever he wanted.

Frank motioned at the wagon. "Let me introduce you to my friend. He's the town blacksmith."

Fargo lifted the reins.

"Pa, look!" Johnny abruptly bawled. "There's Jenny's dog!"

The shout woke the mongrel, which raised its head and sleepily regarded the pair. "Do you know who he belongs to?" Fargo asked.

Frank answered. "Jenny Jeeter. Her mother gave it to her for her birthday a while back. They named him Samson."

"He up and disappeared about five days ago," young Johnny revealed. "Jenny was worried sick. We looked all over, but couldn't find him anywhere."

"I came on him about five miles back," Fargo said. "Had to pry him out of a thicket."

"Five miles?" Frank said, his brow knitting. "That's awful peculiar. He never strays from Jenny's side."

"Not ever," Johnny echoed.

"There's a first time for everything. Maybe he wandered off and got lost," Fargo said. Dogs did it all the time. "I'm on my way into town. I'll drop him off when I get there."

Father and son swapped glances. "You're going into Wolfrik?" Frank said. "There's not much there worth bothering over. If you want, Johnny and I will be more than happy to take Samson in with us and you can go on about your own business."

"I don't mind," Fargo responded. He planned to treat himself to a drink or three and maybe sit in on a few hands of poker.

The stocky man who had been loading saplings into the bed of the wagon came toward them. His store-bought shirt fit too snugly, accenting immensely muscular shoulders and an extremely thick neck. At the sight of Fargo he stopped short. "What do we have here?"

Fargo introduced himself.

"He found Jenny's dog!" Johnny exclaimed.

"Mr. Fargo, this is Luke Barstow," Frank said. "He was one of the first to move to Wolfrik."

"Lucky me," Barstow said, growling the words like an angry beast. "If I'd had any sense I'd have stayed in St.

Louis." He came toward the stallion, a brawny hand outstretched. "Give the dog to me. We'll see that it gets to its rightful owner."

"He says he wants to take Samson in himself," Frank volunteered.

Luke Barstow stopped. "That won't do. You know he can't." Walking to the pinto, Barstow reached for the mongrel's collar.

Fargo couldn't understand what the fuss was about. All he was doing was returning a lost dog. Resting his hand on Samson, he said, "I've brought him this far, I'll take him the rest of the way."

"No, you won't," Barstow persisted, and crooked a thick finger. "Hand him over. Then light a shuck and don't ever show your face in these parts again."

"I'll show my face any damn place I please," Fargo said, annoyed by the blacksmith's gall. He went to ride off but Barstow unexpectedly gripped the stallion's bridle and held on tight.

"Make this easy on yourself, mister. Strangers aren't welcome in Wolfrik. Take my advice and leave while you still can."

"Take *my* advice and mind your own affairs." Sliding his foot from the stirrup, Fargo kicked Barstow's wrist hard enough to force the blacksmith to let go. "And keep your hands off my horse."

Luke Barstow sighed. Then, without any warning whatsoever, he seized Fargo by the ankle and heaved with all his considerable might.

Fargo was upended. He experienced the sensation of falling and felt a jarring impact when his shoulder met the ground. He was up in an instant, raging mad. Samson, unfazed, was still perched on the saddle, slumped in fatigue.

The blacksmith came around the pinto toward him. "I wish there were another way," he said, and waded in with both his massive fists flying.